Travel With Me Through Time
Part II

Theodore Aguilera

Dedicated to
My Mother and Father

Travel With Me Through Time, Part II

© 2013 Theodore Aguilera
All rights Reserved.

Published by Dosey Books
Vacaville, California, U.S.A.

ISBN: 978-0-615-85887-6

Contents

Chapter 1: **An Unwelcome Homecoming**

I have logged many miles now in ole Nelly and I have found her to be much more than a time machine. To me, she is my best friend and faithful travel companion.

From high above San Francisco Bay, I have the whole city in view as I begin my slow descent. My quest is not to save the world, but to have a beer in a bar, any bar. Or maybe two beers—who's counting?

Ah, yes. This place will do nicely. I can taste that delicious golden brew even from in here.

I am able to take ole Nelly down much easier now than when we first started together. I've gotten much better with time, so to speak.

As we settle to the ground, my beautiful craft rises up again just a little bit—about three feet—as the door slowly opens. It swings down to the ground and I step onto the stairs and onto solid earth.

The night air is a little cold, but nothing is better than crisp San Francisco air.

With my door open, I see that the cars, the people and everything else around me have come to a complete stop. All has become frozen with my arrival.

As I disembark, the door starts to close. The time machine settles to the ground and vanishes. I know, though, that it will always come back to me when I call it with my ring.

Like magic, the world returns to life without anyone ever knowing that anything had happened.

I enter the establishment, filled with many people dressed up very fancy—as if to advertise their wealth. Some women wear fur coats, while the men are dressed in fancy thousand-dollar suits, just talking about their money.

Not me, though, because I have no money to talk about.

I just have on a shirt I picked up in Tombstone, Arizona in 1810, some blue jeans and cowboy boots. All Texans wear cowboy boots. It

1

is just the Texas in us. They're good for the bullshit people say to me, and when it gets a bit thick, they help me out every time.

Still, people look at me weird because I don't wear a fancy suit. They may as well just say it to my face. I don't care if they do. It does not bother me one damn bit. I don't try to show off like they do. I am what I am. People are all the same to me, good or bad. I mean, money wouldn't change me in the slightest. If you're ugly then you're ugly and that's it. Fancy clothes aren't going to change anyone no matter what they have on. But people don't seem to get that.

I walk to the bar and see a good place to sit in front of the TV.

There's a picture on the wall of a nude woman on a bed. She looks really hot up there.

The bartender is wearing a white shirt, red coat and black pants. He seems okay to me. He comes over and asks, "What'll it be, sir?"

"I'll have a cold beer. The colder, the better."

"That's what we've got. Coming up, sir."

He brings it to me and I pay the man.

I drink in peace, watching a little TV. This is the life for me. Now I feel like a king.

A little old lady walks by using a cane. It's hard for her to get around from what I can see. She must be eighty-five years old or so, I'd say. I'll bet in her day, she was a wild one. I'll bet she loved to dance out there on the dance floor, too. But time keeps on tick, tick, ticking away for her. This little old lady may have been hot fifty years ago, but no more. She still has her memory to look back on, though. Still, that was then and this is now. Women today never think they'll grow old. But they will, because time keeps on ticking for them, too. They think they have all the time in the world but time is really short for everybody. It may not have caught up to them yet, but it will.

Being a time traveler, I think about time more than most people. I can go back to any time I want and see with my own eyes, anyone when they were young—even this old lady.

A black man with short hair struts in. He wears a light blue suit with light blue shirt and blue shoes. He thinks he's so cool, but really, I'm the only cool one around here.

He stops and gives me a funny look. He then approaches and says, "You're in my favorite seat. You mind getting up so I can watch some TV there, sir?"

Sarcastically, I respond, "Oh, sure. I'm so sorry for sitting in your favorite chair, mister. Please forgive me! It will never happen again. By the way, who appointed you God in here?"

Astonished, he says, "You're crazy. Anyone ever tell you that?"

I say, "I think *you* are the crazy one. Have you seen your doctor today? If not, I think you should—like now. You need some kind of medication and I think you know that."

He gives me another glare and demands, "I want that damn chair and I want it right now or we're going to have a problem!"

"It's not my problem, it's yours."

"I don't want to hear any more of your bullshit! You hear me?"

I respond, "So how long have you thought you were God, mister? I've got some bad news for you. You're not God because I am, sir. If you want my chair, you'll only have to kiss my ass for it." The other customers gasp. "No big deal for you. I'm sure you're used to kissing one now and then. Still, I won't be going out with you on any dates. Are we clear? But I'm all right with a little tongue."

With a dirty look, the big man responds, "Are you talking to me? Because if you are, that's not so good for you. You can get hurt bad talking to me that way. You hear me? You piece of shit! No one ever talks to me like that. You're just asking for it, man, and you will get it from me if you keep it up."

"I don't want to play anymore. Go away, God, or whoever you think you are. And why does everybody want my chair? Do I have a sign on my back that says, 'If you want my chair, please ask'?"

3

He responds, "You don't know who you're talking to, do you—asshole? I'm Mel Maddux, heavyweight champ of the world! I'm the best. You wouldn't last five minutes in the ring with me."

"You're right about that. You'd go down in four. Really, though, you're not the champ because you haven't fought me. *I'm* the best. Oh by the way, isn't 'Mel' a girl's name? I think it is..."

"What's your name, boy?"

"It's not boy. It's Gunnar Best to you."

"Gunnar, you make me laugh—the way you talk to me—because I can kill you with my bare hands and I think you know it."

"Don't count your chickens before they hatch. You think you will win this fight but you'll just be in a whole lot of pain the way I see it. Maybe you'll learn something from this if you keep it up. You think the world should do what you say? I got some news for you. Not true. Not in here with me today. This you can count on from a Texan."

With an icy stare he states, "It's time now to teach you a lesson. Outside, Mr. Best. Are you ready?"

"You seem like a nice guy. I don't feel right about hurting you; knowing you're the heavyweight champ and all that. I tell you what, if you say you're sorry for wanting my chair and about the way you said it, I'll let it go this time. But if we go outside, I will not show you any mercy. But it's your pain, not mine."

"You're too much. I'm going to enjoy this more than you'll ever know, Gunnar. Let's go and see who wins this fight."

"Mel, do you have some coveralls in your car?"

"What? Why?"

"Because when you go down, your new suit will get all dirty. Just trying to help you out here."

If a look could kill, I'd be dead right now.

We go out back, followed by a number of others.

Mel does not know about the watch that John gave me from the planet, Antonion. It has the power to slow down time to the point of stopping it all together. I only need to push a little button.

4

Mel takes off his jacket and passes it to another man. He raises his fists and charges, wanting to murder me with his bare hands. I quickly push the button on the top of my watch. Those around me are starting to slow down. The harder I press, the more time slows for them.

He approaches very slowly while I still move normally. I hit him in the face and many times to his body. He hits the ground hard but gets back up. He tries again but can't make contact. He's just moving too slow for me. Seeing a punch coming, I dodge it without him even touching me. I hit him many times more and he goes down again but this time, cannot get back up. He's hurting bad. The others shout for him to stay down and he finally does.

Using my watch, I return time to normal.

"Sorry, Champ, but it was your call, not mine. I did tell you what would happen. Next time, if someone sits in your chair, just let it go. A chair is not worth it. You know that now."

"How did you beat him?" a man asks.

"Nobody has won here today. He's still the heavy-weight champ of the world." I extend my hand to Mel. Hesitantly, he shakes it and looks to me, astounded. "Let me buy you a beer, Mel. I'll even let you sit in my chair if you want to."

"I could use a beer right now. And a chair, actually. Admittedly, you're a good fighter. Sorry for… you know."

"No reason to be. We're both at fault. I should have just given my chair to you; not fought you for it like I did. If you're sorry, so am I."

We go back into the bar as friends.

He asks me, "Why couldn't I hit you?"

"A friend of mine—John—he taught me what to do in a fight and I simply did what he said."

I know he wants to know more, but it's getting late and I'd rather not discuss it further. "So long, Mel, and good luck out there."

Without my watch, Mel would've killed me. Thanks to my friend, John, for that watch!

I go outside, walk to the corner and look around this big, beautiful city of San Francisco. No wonder so many people love it here. A long time ago, I used to live here, too.

But now it's time to push my ring again and take witness of my glorious time machine. Everything comes to a complete stop. Nothing can move around me—people, cars, everything stops except ole Nelly and myself. All this is like magic to me.

The craft begins rising slowly into the air—about three feet off the ground. My door begins to swing open. Down it goes, allowing me to step up the stairs and into the cockpit. I nestle within my bucket seat as the door starts to close by itself.

What can I do in San Francisco right now for some fun? I know.

We launch up, over the city. Above the bay, I can see everything. I push a button that makes my craft visible to everyone.

Moments later, I see five jets approaching. As they get close, I just slip away from them. They are much too slow to catch me. My time machine can go faster than any other aircraft on this planet. I can blast a hundred miles away and stop on a dime. These jets are like bicycles next to a car going a hundred miles an hour.

Here they come again.

Now I'll just go straight up into the sky. Let's see if they can do that, too. Look at them. So slow in their so-called jets.

Now I have to say good-bye to them. It's been fun but I have to leave. "Let's go home, Nelly. We've had our fun for tonight."

I press the invisibility button and vanish in the sky. I then point Nelly in the direction of my home where I belong.

I'm sure they'll ask, "Where'd it go?" I wonder how many phone calls they'll be getting from people saying they saw me as a UFO.

I see my house up ahead and begin my slow descent. I settle down in my backyard and the door starts to open by itself.

I sit a minute to catch a breath of air and look out the windows. Finally, I rise from my chair and step onto the steps to disembark. As

I turn and look back, my time machine settles down to the ground and vanishes again like always.

Inside, I find my brother, James, in the living room seated next to Debbie, a lovely FBI agent I brought back from 1956 to live with us.

My brother greets me with, "Gunnar, we have to talk."

"What about?"

His eyes tell me that something is very wrong. I turn my gaze to Debbie. She also appears very sad. James finds it difficult to speak.

"Well? I can't take the suspense!"

"Gunnar," he says, "Tom is dead. He was killed two days ago. He was shot around nine o'clock at night in front of his home."

For a moment, I am too shocked to speak.

"I loved him like a brother. What will I do without him?"

"I wish it wasn't so, Gunnar," he says. "You know I loved him, too. We all grew up together. He was a good kid."

Debbie holds me in her arms. "I'm so sorry. I never knew him but I know how much he meant to you. If there's anything I can do—"

"No, I need to be alone right now. Please understand."

I go to the backdoor and open it. I look up at the stars for a brief moment and then walk down the steps slowly to the backyard. I sit on one of our lawn chairs and think about the times we had as kids.

When Tom had cancer, I brought medicine all the way back from the planet Antonion so he would live. Now he's dead anyway.

He and I even talked about getting old together.

Tears stream from my eyes. It takes a lot to make me cry, but he was my best friend. It has been a long time since I cried for someone. The last time was for my mother and father.

I wipe my tears. I look to where my time machine is and wonder why this happened to him—to be gunned down on his own street right outside of his house. I have learned in my time travels to let the dead stay dead. But this is not right.

I push my ring. I walk to my trusted time machine and say to her, "You won't leave me, will you?" Another tear seeps from my eye.

The door starts to open by itself as though ole Nelly were trying to tell me, "Let's go and see what happened to your friend, Gunnar."

I step inside, sit down at the controls and look out the window for a minute. Many things are going through my head. No way will the man who killed my friend live to talk about it! That much I know.

I shout, "Tom, whoever did this, I want you to know he's a dead man! He does not know it yet, but he will be. Let's go, Nelly!"

Chapter 2: **Revenge**

I program my dashboard computer for two days ago, 9:00 pm. I'm determined to see what really happened to my friend, Tom.

I initiate my return back in time.

I stop ole Nelly on the sidewalk in front of his home. From here, I can see everything coming and going.

At the moment, there's nobody around, so I wait.

I see Tom walking up the street, not knowing that death waits for him in just a few minutes.

The last time we spoke, I came to help him with a weight problem he had developed since high school. He looks a lot thinner now.

A man abruptly steps in front of him from the shadows and pulls a gun from his coat. Tom looks at the man with eyes wide.

I can't quite make out their words, but it seems clear that this man wants Tom's money.

Tom goes in his pocket and pulls out his wallet. He gives it to the man and then raises his hands. Through my window, I can barely hear Tom nervously saying, "That's all I got, sir."

The robber responds, "Think I'm going to let you snitch me out? I'm not that stupid."

"What? Hold on! I won't tell anyone! You have my word! Please don't take the rest of my life away. I still have too much living to do. Please, let me live it out!"

"No deal. It's *my* life here on the line. Sorry, mister, but you are going to die today." He strikes Tom in the face with his gun.

Tom falls to the ground, gets back up and wipes the blood off his mouth. I can see that he's mad but there's nothing he can do about it.

"Every man I kill, I hit across the face. It's like me saying to them, 'Good-bye from me to you.'"

"If you kill me, I know that my friend, Gunnar, will not stop until he finds you and kills you! I promise you that. So you, too, will die if you kill me. Count on it! There is nowhere you can hide from him. So let me go and you will also live."

"Your friend won't find me because he doesn't know who I am!"

The man shoots Tom twice and his body slumps to the ground.

Tom mumbles, "Gunnar…" His last breath gives out and he dies.

The anguish it causes me to see this! The frustration! Yet, I can do nothing. I want desperately to prevent this. Still, John from Antonion warned me of this very thing. I know to always let the dead be dead. It just has to be that way.

"So much for your friend," the man says as he kicks Tom's body. He looks like he enjoyed that, too, as he leaves him there like some kind of dead animal.

Within my time machine, I follow this man. Where he goes, I go. In here, I can pass through any objects in my way. I am only five feet away from this guy who thinks he just got away with killing my best friend. But he won't get away with anything. I saw it all happen in front of my own two eyes. He has no idea that I'm right here watching every move he makes.

He goes into a liquor store, two blocks away. He looks so satisfied with the money in his pocket he got from killing my friend. He peers around to see if anyone is watching and goes to some magazines and picks one up. The sight of a naked woman on its cover puts a smile on his face. "Oh, yeah, momma," he says. He takes it to the counter.

He glares at the man behind the counter and sets down the goods.

"That all for you, sir?" the clerk asks.

"What more could a man want? Except a bottle of whisky, too. Oh—I almost forgot—and a pack of them cigarettes. Got to have my cigarettes. You know how it is."

"I sure do."

He goes into his pocket, pays the man with Tom's money and then leaves the store. He walks a while, then hops into a car and drives off. Not knowing that I'm behind him all the way, he parks and goes into his house like nothing special had happened today.

I follow.

He doesn't know it yet, but when the time is right, he's dead.

Entering the living room, two small children run to him with hugs and kisses. The boy, about five, wears brown shorts and a white shirt. The girl, nine, wears a beautiful white dress. She couldn't look more adorable. They appear to love their father very much and are actually well behaved from what I can see so far.

His wife enters from the kitchen in a summer dress with a pattern of many flowers. She is so beautiful. "Dinner's ready," she says. How did he get a woman like that? She has long blonde hair and a beautiful body that any man would desire.

They eat as I sit in my time machine and watch.

After dinner, he goes into the living room and watches some TV. A few moments pass and he gets out the magazine he bought earlier and looks it over. He gets up and goes to the kitchen for a glass. His wife is there washing dishes. "I'm going to bed after I'm done," she says. "Don't be up late." He drags himself back to his chair and starts drinking the whiskey he bought with Tom's money not long ago.

He continues to drink for a while, occasionally looking over to the stairs where his wife now heads up for bed. He studies her soft body intently as she takes each step. He takes another swig. It's apparent that he's getting a little drunk. He finally puts down the magazine and drinks the last of his booze. He appears to have only one thing on his mind as he heads upstairs. He stops, though, and staggers back to get his magazine before resuming.

Reaching the second floor he yells, "Honey! It's your husband and you know what I want! You better have your clothes off for me by the time I get in there! Hear me, baby? Better do as I say, woman."

He finds the bedroom door, however, locked.

"Let me in there, Honey! You're my wife and have to do as I say. You hear me? Give me some of that good sex I want from you! And I want it now! You hear me, woman?"

"Harry," she shouts, "you know you have had too much to drink. Please go to sleep downstairs tonight."

"No! Not tonight, baby. I need sex, woman! You knew that when I married you."

"Please do this for me because you love me, okay?"

You have a good ass and nice tits. That's what I love. That's what I married you for. I need it bad right now so give it! Help me out."

"No, Harry. Not tonight. Please go downstairs and go to sleep!"

He slams his shoulder into the door and breaks it down.

The children can't help but hear the commotion and come out into the hall. "Get back in your room!" he orders, but they do not comply. They are frightened and are worried for their mother. He takes off his belt and starts whipping them. Crying, they retreat to their room.

He bursts into his bedroom and smacks his wife across the face. "Look what you made me do—hit our children because you wouldn't open the damn door for me!"

He tears off her clothes and throws her onto the bed like she was a whore and not his wife. He gazes upon her naked body as though she were nothing but a piece of meat.

"You're hurting me, Harry! Please stop!"

"I don't care! You know why? Because you made me hit our kids. And I like it!"

While on top of her, he lays his magazine over her head and turns the pages during intercourse, striking her occasionally.

"You like that, woman?"

When he's done, he tells her, "Honey, you were real good, baby. Real good. I'm glad I married you."

Finally, he passes out. The magazine falls onto the floor, its pages turning until finally coming to rest.

Watching the whole thing, I chose to do nothing. What they do in their bedroom is none of my business. I have one objective here and that is to kill the man who killed my best friend.

As his wife lies there sobbing, I decide to return the next evening when Harry is sober.

I locate them in the kitchen. "You really hurt me last night!" she complains. "My breasts are in a lot of pain. And just look at my face! Why did you hit me like that?"

"I don't know why, but you have my word, I won't hit you again. I see those naked girls in those magazines and when I get to drinking, it turns me into an animal. You're such a beautiful woman and when I see you, it turns me on so much and I couldn't stop myself. I told you I'm sorry. What more can I do?"

"You can go to the store and buy bread for tomorrow's lunch."

The children come in and still appear uneasy. His daughter asks, "Why did you hit us last night, Daddy?"

He bends down and says, "It was your mother's fault, not mine. She locked the door and wouldn't open it so I had to break it down. Otherwise, I couldn't go to bed." He looks to his wife. "Right, dear?"

Hesitantly, she responds, "Yes, it was my fault, not your father's. Go brush your teeth now."

Confused, the children leave.

She gives her husband an icy stare. "You know, Harry, sometimes I wish I never married you. Sometimes I which you were dead."

He walks menacingly toward her. She flinches as he grabs her but it is merely a kiss that he delivers this time. "Oh, you don't mean that, Honey. You know you love me too much. You know you do."

She turns from him and goes to the next room.

Harry says, "Okay, Honey, I'll go to the store and get some bread for you now… because I love you so much and you have a nice ass."

He heads outside and hops into his car and drives off. Arriving at the market, he finds a place to park around the corner and climbs out into the dark neighborhood. There is no one else around.

About five feet from his car, I open the door to my time machine. Everything stops moving, including this man who shot my best friend. I get out and go to my trunk. I take out one of the firearms I got back in Tombstone; the one I will use to finish this scum once and for all. I close my door and everything resumes. Stunned, Harry looks at me and the gun I have pointed at him.

"Where did you come from?"

I say nothing, glaring at him for a tense minute.

Shaking, he says, "Take all my money if you want it. Just take it but don't kill me. I have a wife and children!"

"I don't want your money, Harry, and I don't care about your wife and children. What I do want is your life. Do you know who I am?"

"No. That's the truth! I honestly don't!" Puzzled, he then asks, "Hey, how do you know my name?"

"That's not important. My name is Gunnar Best, the man who will kill you today. You killed my best friend, remember? He told you that if you killed him, I would find you and kill you no matter where you went. I did find you and I will kill you now just like you robbed and killed my best friend."

"I didn't kill anybody! You got me mixed up with someone else!"

"No, it was you all right. I know that to be true because I saw you do it so don't lie to me!"

"How can you be so sure it was me?"

"If you must know, I have a time machine. Once I found out that someone had killed my best friend, I went back and watched you kill him and that's how I know, Harry."

He starts to grin but looks again at the pistol in my hand and the expression on my face. "Yes, all right. I'm sorry for what I did to your friend. Let's call the police! I'll tell them what I did and go to jail if it'll make you happy."

"We're beyond all that. My friend told you he wanted to live, too, and all you said was, 'Sorry, mister, but you are going to die today.'"

"How do you know all this?"

"Oh yeah, and one more thing…" I strike him in the face with my gun and he falls to the ground.

14

"What about my wife and kids? Please don't kill me. Let me live! What you're doing here is murder!"

"Why is this called murder, but it's not murder when you took my best friend's life? Tell me, I'd like to know, asshole!"

"But what about my family?"

"I know all about your wife and your kids! But you murdered the wrong man yesterday. After you're dead, I'm going to your house on 1412 Adam Street and show your pretty wife my gun and my knife."

His eyes grow wide.

"I'm going to slice up your little boy and your daughter and mix their pieces together. I think that will be a lot of fun. First, though, I look forward to watching them die slowly in front of me. Then I will screw your pretty wife—all day long—and will kill her if she doesn't do as I say. You'll be dead, so you won't be able to save them. When I'm done with her, I'll just kill her, too. How about that, Harry? It's going to be a good day for me."

"Please don't hurt my family! Kill me, but not my kids! My wife's a good woman. I'll do anything you want!"

"Your wife is better off without you. She said that this morning. Didn't you hear?"

He looks at me with shock.

"I'm like you, Harry. I've kill before and I'll kill again. It's no big deal to me. I'll give you two minutes and then you die, piece of shit."

He goes down to the ground, mumbling about his wife and kids. Abruptly, he pulls a gun and fires two shots at me. The bullets stop an inch away from my body and fall to the ground. I carry a *revealer*, which lets me move while everyone else stays frozen in time and acts as a protective shield against anything that may try to harm me.

Defeated, he knows what is about to happen to him.

"Good-bye, Harry." I fire three shots into his chest.

I say softly, "That was for you, Tom. I hope you feel better now. And don't worry; I won't harm his wife and kids. I just wanted him to suffer for what he did to you."

15

I press my ring and my time machine is there looking at me as its doors start to open. I enter, sit and look out the windows. It's hard to kill a man with a wife and kids but what else could I do? Now she has no husband and the children no father. Still, he would've killed again and again. He had to be stopped and so I stopped him.

I just sit and think about how cruel people can be. Sometimes they just make me sick. I need to get away for a while. I need to be alone to get my head on straight and have some time to myself.

I know. I'll go back to before there were any people at all. I'll go back, say, sixty million years before man came to be.

The study of dinosaurs was a favorite subject of mine when I was a kid. I could even name most of them.

I set the controls.

"Let's go back, ole Nelly, to before there were any people at all."

Chapter 3: **Before Man**

I start to see things changing outside of my time machine. They go by so fast—houses, cars and people—until finally the city is no more.

"So long, brother James. I'll miss you—but out here is no man's land. No one here but me, your baby brother—the only man alive."

I look up to the sky and see the moon and stars going around and around. The many days and nights pass so quickly. I could never hope to count them all.

There's only me and ole Nelly passing through time. I see nothing but naked land before me now.

Snow begins to collect all around us. Soon, I can no longer see because my windows are covered in snow and ice. It is dark in here until the lights come on by themselves. It's getting a little cold, too. I should have brought a coat. Nelly then begins putting out some heat. I know she cares for me. She knows I'm only human. This must be the Great Ice Age.

The snow starts to dissipate. I can see out the windows again.

Molten rock starts to form around my craft. Now it's getting a bit warm in here.

I'm seriously considering taking some clothes off when the time machine begins cooling me down. I should be cooked alive right now in this pool of hot lava, which is not hurting my time machine at all. Whoever built this thing sure did a fantastic job. Thank God for you, whoever you are. I owe you one!

Time continues backwards. Eventually, it begins to slow. Now the lava hardly seems to be moving at all. According to the computer on my dashboard, millions of years have gone by.

The lava levels go down, but very slowly. There is a giant volcano to my right. It looks like an enormous mountain from here. It erupts. Man, the Earth just seems like one red ball of fire. I don't see how anything can possibly live here.

Fifty million years have gone by. I'm the only man alive. Just me, the Texan. There are no homes outside or people walking about.

Plant life begins to return. It's starting to look beautiful again.

The Earth where I lived no longer exists.

We stop at sixty million years ago, but to me, it's still today.

"Nelly, let's go and look around." I move us forward.

I hear noise up ahead and go see what it is. A Tyrannosaurus Rex! A big one, too. I'd say forty feet long and about eight tons.

His eyes look fiery red and thirsty for blood but I feel safe here in my time machine.

He turns his head toward me, however, like he knows I am here. He can't see me, that I know, but I can tell in his eyes that he knows I am somewhere close by. He sniffs around in my direction, looking for his next meal. Snapping his huge jaws, he certainly smells something. He tries for another bite but his big teeth just go right through me and my time machine. It's time to move on.

Wow! He's following me! I speed up but he begins to sprint. As I move faster, he moves a little faster, too. I stop and he stops. We both know I am here. This primitive animal is actually far more perceptive of my presence than any of the modern humans and their technology from my time!

He stops and sees something else to eat. A triceratops. He strikes and bites onto its neck with his sharp teeth. With his powerful jaws, he rips it apart. In the eyes of this triceratops, it seems to understand that the T-rex is hungry but would very much like to go on living! Yet the T-rex persists and this animal will now feel no more pain.

I've never seen anything like this before—one animal eating other and me so close.

But I have seen enough. This is making me sick to my stomach. I take ole Nelly through some rocks and plants up ahead.

Some of these trees seem like early versions of oak, walnut and maple. Over there looks like a forest, a good place for animals to hide from others who really want to eat them.

18

"Let's go on and take a look, Nelly. This old world is all so new to me and you, old girl."

I see water and more dinosaurs drinking there. I see iguanodons. Some are eating. Some stand while others are on all fours. Amazing! I move a little closer for a better look. They can bend their little fingers to grasp twigs and leaves. I never knew that.

I think my home is in the water, if this is sixty million years ago. It looks so clean as it moves into that big lake below.

Abruptly, all the dinosaurs begin running together down the river. There's why. A large, meat-eating dinosaur has come to drink.

I'll move on to the lake and see what's going on there.

Here, before my eyes, are the largest animals I've ever imagined. They have very long necks. Some stand upright to reach leaves on the tops of giant trees. They walk, though, on all fours. They must weigh a hundred tons! I believe the species is called "diplodocus."

Nearby is a dinosaur eating another dinosaur. It seems to have had enough and so it just walks away, leaving the rest. Scavengers quickly descend on the remains and feast until another large dinosaur picks up the scent and scares them off.

To my left are some very pretty flowers. I think I'll pick some for Debbie. She is, after all, a woman and every woman likes flowers no matter what. She'll really like these because they're rare, as in, sixty million years extinct. How many lucky women ever get flowers like that from a nice guy like me?

I maneuver ole Nelly closer to the flowers and we come to a halt. My door starts to open and everything out there stops moving.

I better load both of my guns before I go outside—just in case.

Outside, before me, is what I believe is a coelophysis—a dinosaur about three feet high and ten feet long. What nice teeth it has. I place my hand upon its motionless body. It feels like a lizard to the touch.

I look around and hop on this dinosaur like a small horse and yell, "Yee-ha! Let's go, boy!"

But it's time to get to work, so I get off of this dinosaur-horse of mine and begin picking some flowers for Debbie. I know she's going to love them. There sure are a lot of these out here and they do smell very good. I place them on the passenger seat and go back for more.

Bringing back a second batch, I step into a hole and stumble to the ground. My ring strikes against a rock, which causes the door to start closing as my time machine vanishes before my eyes. I stand back up and urgently press my ring, which seems stuck in the down position.

Hearing movement all around me, I look about, knowing millions of dinosaurs are out here wanting to eat me. I'm in trouble now, even if exposed for just a few seconds, I'm a dead man.

No sooner said, numerous beasts begin to converge around me, including the one I was just riding a minute ago. It looks at me like dinner is here. He strides hastily in my direction. It's now a matter of pulling out my gun even quicker or becoming a meal for this ancient predator. I draw my pistol and shoot. With two shots to the head, it goes down, though the others keep coming. I redirect my fire at the next one as yet another bursts forth and halts at the sound of my weapon. I'm out of bullets now and have no time to reload. I look at the dinosaur and he looks at me with ravenous hunger in his eyes.

I raise my empty pistol, and this savage hunter takes a step closer. I then slam it against my ring.

Just when I think I'm done for, ole Nelly returns to save my ass. She's my girl and that's why I love her! Time freezes, making a big statue of that dinosaur that almost had me for a snack.

Jack, the Earthman who gave me this time machine, taught me to always know how many bullets you have in your gun. He said that my life would someday depend on it. I failed on this point today and it almost cost me my ass. That was way too close for comfort.

Next to me, I study this frozen dinosaur that looks just like the Devil himself. He's red and black with little horns all over his head. One day, they will name him "pachycephalosaurus." What a name.

I get back inside my time machine. With a push of a button, I am invisible again.

There is a thunderous sound and the ground shakes. Massive trees begin to sway violently all around me. My time machine, however, is off the aground about three feet so I remain stable. A volcano erupts, hurling giant, hot rocks into the air. Trees topple and boulders tumble over the hills. Down the mountainside, lava flows into the valley.

The dinosaurs are running for their lives with no hope in sight.

It's time to get back home! I set the controls for 2011 and hit the green button. I begin moving forward in time and watch as this world of the dinosaur comes to an end.

We become engulfed in lava. No car or anything else could take what my time machine is taking this moment from Mother Earth. My craft grows very hot but remains cool inside because ole Nelly likes me and does her best to keep me alive.

The lava and rock dissipate after a few million years, so says my dashboard computer.

I look to the sky for the last time in this ancient age. The planet is changing. Snow falls again as Nelly and I pass in and out through The Great Ice Age together.

I did learn one thing from the dinosaurs. Living there was a matter of kill or be killed. Only the strong can survive. That's life, I guess.

I reset my controls for 9:00 pm, the day before Tom was killed.

I load more bullets into my gun as we arrive in the city.

I find the man who is to kill Tom, waiting for him to come home. I climb out of my time machine, approach him and declare, "You, sir, must die." I pull my gun and shoot him down like the dog that he is.

Squirming on the ground he asks, "Why'd you shoot me like that? I would've given you my money!"

"I don't want your money. I did it to keep you from murdering my best friend. I'm sure others would have died because of you, too. It's for the best. I know that now. And it was the right choice to make."

He says, "I have a wife and kids. Did you know that before you shot me? You're killing me for nothing, you psycho!"

"I know about your family. Your wife is a very beautiful woman. She will not have a tough time finding a new husband. I might even marry her myself—who knows? Either way, it'll work out."

He dies like an animal. I won't lie; it felt good to kill him.

"Rest in peace, you piece of shit."

His killing days are now over. They stop here for good.

I never killed anyone like that before. But it had to be done so my friend could live on to be an old man with me.

The law couldn't help with this. There's a time when a man must be a man and take the law into his own hands for the good of others.

Harry's house is just a few doors down, across the street.

His wife comes outside and looks about. As we make eye contact, I open the door to my time machine and she no longer moves. I climb in and close the door, resuming time to normal. She finds her husband lying face down on the ground. She breaks down and rushes to him. Holding him in her arms, she can't stop crying.

"I am sorry, young lady, but it had to be done."

It's time for me to head back home.

"Let's go, Nelly. We just did something good for a lot of people on this day. Even her."

Chapter 4: **A Flower's Allure**

Arriving back home, I set Nelly down in the backyard and remain seated, resting in my bucket seat, thinking of the lady whose husband I just killed. I wish I could tell her how bad I feel about it and why I did it. But either he lives or Tom dies. I think I made the right choice.

Letting out a sigh, I get up and disembark.

Entering my house, I look around the living room and note that it looks the same as before I went back to the time of the dinosaur.

My brother, James, looks up from today's newspaper and tells me, "Oh, Tom just phoned about a half-hour ago."

He doesn't suspect a thing about Tom's death, which I prevented. I'll always know, but will never speak of what really happened.

"What did he want?"

"Call him back and find out."

I take out my phone and head up to my room, dialing on the way. "Hi, Tom. What's happening with you?"

"Oh, nothing ever happens to me, Gunnar. You know that."

"You never know what can happen to you in this world of ours."

"Don't ask me why," he says, "but I had to hear your voice again. Something inside just wanted to say thanks for being my buddy."

"Yeah, I get it, Tom—more than you'll ever know. I have to take a nap right now but thanks for calling. Good-bye and live long for me, my friend." Gratified, I hang up and head back downstairs.

"Where's Debbie?" I ask my brother.

"Dining room."

Indeed, she is there. "Debbie, I've got some flowers here for you. I know you'll like them because all women do."

"Oh, they're gorgeous! I love them, Gunnar!"

"How would you like to go out to dinner with me tonight?" I ask. "Maybe some music and dancing, too. How's that sound?"

"I thought you'd never ask."

"Tonight will be our night, then. I just need to get some sleep first. How about eight o'clock?"

"Sounds good to me," she says.

At 7:30, I get up and put on my best suit. I know she'll like that.

I find Debbie in the living room, all prettied up with one of those flowers in her hair and another on her stunning black dress. I could kiss her right here and now but my brother is watching.

"You sure don't look like an FBI agent. You look like the most beautiful woman in the whole damn world. Let's have a good time." To James I yell, "Don't wait up. No telling when we'll be home!"

"Have fun."

At the restaurant, the hostess shows us to our table and the waiter soon arrives. "What would you like to drink tonight?" he asks. I look at Debbie's beautiful face and say, "A fine bottle of wine, sir, for me and this beautiful young lady."

She and I talk for a bit until the music begins to play. I look at her tonight not as a friend or an agent of the FBI, but as a lovely woman.

"A beautiful restaurant, a beautiful woman and beautiful music. It would be a sin not to dance. Shall we? The music belongs to us."

She smiles, stands and gives me her hand.

While holding each other on the dance floor, a woman passes us, unable to keep her eyes off of Debbie.

When the music stops, we go back to our table.

The curious lady soon approaches. "Sorry to interrupt," she says, "but where did you get those beautiful flowers in your hair?"

Debbie responds, "I don't know where they came from. My friend here gave them to me."

I say, "If I told you where I got them, you would not believe me."

"Of course I would. Please tell me."

"Well, I didn't steal them, if you must know. Why so interested? A flower is just a flower to me."

"I ask because those flowers you have don't exist anymore. They went extinct millions of years ago—or so I thought."

24

"To me, they are simply special flowers for a special lady."

Debbie smiles and groans.

The woman says, "The fact is, sir, those flowers were thought to have grown when dinosaurs roamed the Earth. Did you know that?"

"Now that you mention it, I do know something about dinosaurs. They make bad horses to ride on.

"But when I first saw those flowers, I thought of Debbie. I knew she would like them. She is someone special to me and she knows it. If you'll excuse us for now, please."

"Of course," she hesitantly responds.

Debbie and I soon return to the dance floor. She feels so good in my arms; like a woman should feel in the arms of a man.

A bit later, the lady and her husband approach our table.

"I'm very sorry to disturb you again, but I just needed my husband to see your lovely flowers. Do you mind?"

I'm getting a bit annoyed now but I smile and nod.

The man inspects the petals closely. "My word! It's true. Sir, you must tell us where you found these."

"Sir," I tell him, "my friend and I are trying to enjoy our evening together. We didn't come to talk about flowers with you or your wife. This night belongs to us lovebirds. Do you understand?"

"Of course I do. I was young once myself."

"Look, if it's okay with Debbie, I'll give you one of her flowers so you can give it to your wife. Will that make you happy?"

Debby says, "I'd be glad to." She removes one from her dress and hands it to the man's wife.

"Happy now?"

The man asks, "What about that other one in her hair?"

I glare at the man and say, "Sir, you're too much. You know that? We'll give you her other flower, too, but only if you and your wife promise to leave us alone."

"I'm sorry. Yes of course."

Debbie hands over the other flower with some reluctance.

I tell her, "I have lots more waiting for you at home. In a week or two they'll all be dead and in the garbage anyway."

The man looks to me with interest. "You know, I love garbage so very much. I'd be glad to pick up yours for you if you want me to."

"You like garbage? You don't look like a man who likes garbage to me. You seem too intelligent."

"Not true! Please, though, don't mix your other garbage with the flowers. They are so delicate. That would just break my heart."

"Do you like cutting lawns, too?" I ask. "My brother always wants me to cut the lawn. If you'd rather do it instead, I could give you my address. If not, there'd be no reason to give it to you, I suppose."

"Would that really be necessary?" he asks.

"Well, if you were to come over and cut our lawn and if you got thirsty, you could come inside and drink some water and look at all the other different kinds of extinct flowers we have."

Quickly, he responds, "I love to cut lawns, too, sir!"

"How much would you charge me for cutting my lawn?"

Debbie gives me a bothered look.

He says "Oh, I would just do it for the fun of it. Not one red cent."

"Me, too," his wife adds. "I love the smell of fresh-cut grass!"

I write down my address and hand it to him.

"So we have a deal. Can you come tomorrow in the morning? My brother won't be home and I want to show him what a hard worker I am if you know what I mean."

"Yes," the woman says as she takes the paper from her husband.

They head back to their table. Neglecting their dinner all together, they simply stare at the flowers we had given them.

I ask Debbie, "How about another dance?"

"Sure."

As we twirl to the fast music, the old couple watches. I know they have a thousand questions for us.

"Gunnar," Debbie says, "you're taking advantage of those elderly people and you know it. To make them throw your garbage out and cut your lawn? That's too much. I want you to go over there right now and invite them for dinner at seven, instead."

"But I'm dancing right now with you, my sweet, and I am a good dancer; you know that."

She immediately stops and looks at me with those beautiful blue eyes, which break me down. I just want you to know that, I'm only doing this for you, Debbie."

I turn from her and walk over to the couple. They look to me with question and great interest.

"My lady friend has asked me to tell you not to come over and cut our lawn but to come for dinner tomorrow at seven instead. Though, if you still want to cut my grass, that's okay with me, too."

The man says, "I lied. I don't like to cut grass at all."

"Me neither," his wife says with a grin. "I hate that smell of grass. See you at seven."

"Fine. Well will be expecting you promptly at seven o'clock.

After an evening of dancing and talking, Debbie and I head home. Inside, I don't see my brother. He must already be in bed.

I sit down in the living room and Debbie sits near on the couch.

The way she's acting and looking at me is different from when we first met in her time of 1956.

"Come sit closer to me, Gunnar. I don't bite."

I slowly get up and sit by her side. I look into her eyes and see a woman there, not just Debbie my friend.

"You know, Gunnar, I really like your name. Such a man's name. And you really know how to act like a man. Women like that."

"Good to know."

"And you were right about flowers. They touch a woman deep in her heart. They say to her, 'I love you.'

"Remember," she continues, "in that hotel in '56? You asked if I liked your body and if I wanted to make love to you but I said 'no'?"

"Uh-huh."

"Well, I wanted to say 'yes' but I couldn't. It's a girl thing. We're not supposed to say 'yes' to every man that wants us. But you do have a nice, strong body that any woman would love to make love to."

"Debbie, can I kiss you and make love to you?"

"What's holding you back? It's not me. Don't talk about it, just do whatever you want."

I kiss her soft lips that taste so good; something I've wanted to do since the first time I saw her. Now it's finally happening. I can't keep my hands off her! I feel like an animal that's just found its mate.

Debbie tears the shirt from my back and starts kissing me all over. She looks upon my bare chest and tells me, "Let's go to my bedroom. We don't want to wake your brother, do we?"

We get up and walk to her bedroom. She shuts the door.

You know that saying, "What happens in Vegas, stays in Vegas"? The same holds true here. Sorry, maybe next time.

At seven o'clock the next evening, the couple from the restaurant arrives at our house, right on time.

"You have a beautiful home here," the woman comments.

She wears a dark blue dress with a flower pattern. Her husband is in a light brown coat and pants with white shirt. They even brought a bottle of wine.

My brother joins us in the living room.

"Here is my brother, James. James this is... well, how about that! I don't even know your names! I am Gunnar Best and our flower girl, here, is Debbie."

Debbie gives me a smile. I think she's still happy from last night.

The man responds, "I am Adam Taylor and this is my wife and best friend, Ashley. We're researches at the California Academy of Sciences over in Golden Gate Park in the paleontology department, studying life from the age of dinosaurs."

Ashley sees some of the flowers I've laid out on the table. "These are incredible!" she says. "And what a variety! I have never seen this flower alive before; only in fossil form."

28

Debbie asks, "Would you like one for your hair?" To the men she says, "It's a girl thing."

"How many will you let me have?"

"As many as you want," Debbie says. "Make yourself look pretty for your husband."

Ashley turns to me, wondering if I would object, and then looks to her husband and says, "Just one would be fine."

"Think about it," I say. "More flowers make one more beautiful. And each flower is millions of years old. Can you hear time ticking away back to the dinosaur age? When you get back home, you'll say to yourself, 'I should have put more flowers in my hair when I had the chance!' But by then, it'll be too late to go back in time and do this."

"You're right," she responds. "My beauty is very important to me and my husband so I'll take a few more if that's okay."

"They're only flowers to me," I tell her. "I am a man and you are a woman. Flowers mean a lot more to you."

"You may not believe this, Gunnar," Ashley says, "but at one time my husband and I were hippies. I used to wear flowers in my hair all the time and Adam, here, had hair longer than mine!"

"That is pretty hard to imagine!"

Adam says, "It's true. Back in the 1960s, we believed in free love, lived with a bunch of other hippies and slept with different people at the same time. Heck, that's how Ashley and I met in the first place. Opposing the Vietnam War, we rebelled against society, developing our own style of dress and behavior. But that was a long time ago."

"Well, how about we have some dinner now," I suggest.

We head into the dining room and Adam opens the bottle of wine. "This is my favorite wine. When you taste it, you will know why. It's my last bottle, too. I want you to enjoy it as much as we have enjoyed the flowers you have given us.

"The other night, my wife asked me to take her out to dinner. To be honest, I didn't really want to go. However, now I am really glad I did because here we are now with you nice people."

"I'll drink to that," James says and we all raise our glasses.

Halfway into dinner, he says to me, "Brother, what's the deal with the lawn? You said you were going to cut it last week."

"Yeah, I did say that. I was working on it, but something came up with Debbie."

"What does Debbie have to do with the lawn being cut?"

"It's a long story."

Mr. Taylor says, "I do have an answer to the lawn question. I have a fellow who does my own landscaping. I'll tell him to do yours, too. And please don't say 'no.' I'd like to do this for you nice people."

"I would never think of saying 'no' to you, Mr. Taylor. I wouldn't want to hurt your feelings. It is perfectly fine with me to let your man come over and cut our lawn. Mighty nice of you."

James seems almost disappointed but says nothing.

After dinner, the men go into the living room. Ashley and Debbie stay behind with the flowers, making Ashley look pretty.

"Okay, so I have to ask you, Gunnar," Adam says. "Where in the world did you get those flowers?"

"Adam, today you and your wife hit the jackpot and you know it. You have flowers that are millions of years old; all at no cost to you. You should be happy with that."

"Of course we're grateful, but—"

"Adam, I have a friend named Jack. He told me once never to tell anybody about such things as these flowers I have given you. He said people will not stop searching for more and more. In the end, I think it's better to just let it end here and leave it at that."

"Your friend is wise. It's true. People are never happy with what they have. But I'm happy with the flowers you have given us and I thank you for that."

"You know, Adam, the flowers you have there will produce seed, from which more flowers will grow. With just what you have, you'll be a famous man one day. Wait and see. Only please keep my name out of it. You can keep all the glory for yourself and your wife."

30

His wife walks in with many flowers in her hair. She looks like a young schoolgirl. "Those look very good on you," I tell her. "Debbie, you did a good job on Mrs. Taylor there."

"I think it's time to go," Adam says. "I thank you for everything; especially the flowers. You don't know what they mean to our work."

"Good night, you two," Debbie says as they walk out of the house.

After they're gone, I sit around with Debbie and James and say, "You know, so many things have happened to me recently."

"Like what?" James asks.

"Well, since Jack gave me his time machine, I have gone back to 1914 and met some nice women—Candy and Clara. Jack showed me how to use a gun there in The Wild West, too. Then, I went back to 1980, saw my mother and father and then met you, Debbie, in 1956. Met some other lovely women, too. From there, I went to a few other planets and even saved a few astronauts' lives."

Debbie asks, "So where *did* you get those flowers?"

"Oh, from our backyard, practically. I just went back about sixty million years. I had to fight off a dinosaur for them but I won out with my gun. If I hadn't, I would've been its dinner.

"No telling where I'll go next. But for now, I'll just go to bed."

Chapter 5: **The Fountain of Youth**

In the morning, I get up and get dressed. I go downstairs and find Debbie and my brother in the kitchen drinking coffee.

"Who wants to go downtown with me?" I ask. "Anybody? What about you, Debbie? You up for a good walk?"

"I'm a working woman. You know that, Gunnar."

"What about you, brother? You are getting a little fat there."

"I don't like to walk. I've told you a million times. I have a car. It does all that walking for me. And I'm not getting fat. You just want someone to go walking with you."

"Well, then, I guess I'll just go again by myself. Bye, everyone."

I head down Hilltop Drive to my favorite restaurant.

I see a young woman washing her car. She was doing that the last time I came by. I sure do love pretty ladies.

She sees me approaching and says, "Hello there. How's the world been treating you since I last saw you?"

"It's been an adventure."

"Hey, I've been in your home. It's very cool. Your brother, James, let me in. Does he have a girlfriend?"

"Uh, not that I know of."

"Good."

"Well," I tell her, "good-bye."

She is so hot! Why she would like my brother over me, though, is a mystery. That's life, I guess.

Reaching the restaurant, I see not too many customers here today, which is good for getting a decent table. There are some ladies eating near the counter, however, which is nice. I always like to see women. I sit close to a window so I can look out at this beautiful day going by.

The waiter arrives with a smile and asks if I'm ready.

"I will have some coffee—I need it real bad—and a piece of pie; anything will do as long as it's pie."

"Well, okay! I'll be right back with that coffee you need so badly and a piece of pie."

A young man approaches my table. It seems as if he knows me, judging by the look on his face.

"Hi, Gunnar. How are you today? May I sit? There is something I would like to discuss."

"Do I know you?"

"In a way, yes. In another way, no. But I do know you, Gunnar, very well. You could say I've known you a very long time now."

"And what do you mean by that?"

"If I might sit, I can tell you my story—about where we first met for starters."

"Fine. This better be good, though, or you're out of here."

The waiter arrives with my coffee and pie. He looks at this other man sitting with me and asks, "Can I get you something, sir?"

"I'll just have a cup of coffee—black."

As the waiter departs, the man says, "What I am about to say, you may not believe. But, Gunnar... I cannot die. I will live forever. I will even outlive you someday. You should know this before I begin. My condition is why I am here. You are the only one who can help me."

"How can I help you?"

"My name is Pedro Lorenzo. I was in Tombstone when you and Jack killed a man named 'Billy.' I saw the whole thing back in 1810. You two came into the bar drinking whiskey. You sat and Billy came to your table and demanded that you sit elsewhere. Like I said, I have known you for a long time now.

"I was sitting in that restaurant in Berkeley in 1956 when you met a couple of girls named 'Rose' and 'Mary.' They were nice looking. I saw the way Rose looked at you and I heard Mary tell you she would make love to you in her home if you let her. Seems she did not care how Rose felt about it. Sounded like a pretty good deal to me.

"Now you have Debbie. She's a nice one, too. I like her."

"How do you know all this, Pedro?"

34

"It is a long story but I know you have time to listen."

The waiter returns with my order and gives Pedro his coffee.

"Gunnar, I know you have a machine that lets you travel through time. I need it so I can go back to my era."

Acting shocked, I say, "A time machine? I don't know what you are talking about. Is this something that makes coffee real fast?"

"You are wise to keep it a secret, and I understand that, but that will not work with me. Why waste my time and yours? We both know you have a machine that can take us back."

"I still don't know what you're talking about, Mr. Lorenzo. Is this time machine a clock of some kind?"

"Mr. Gunner Best, I will make it easy for you to understand me. That is the name you gave to Max The Great. Remember that day? He put you under hypnosis back in 1956. I was there at the show. I heard you say that you were a time traveler. Mary and Rose heard it as well. I was sitting in the front row so you cannot dismiss this."

"All right, Pedro. What is it you want?"

"Like I told you, my story is a long one. But, if you are to believe, you should hear it. I was once a sailor, many years ago. It was March, 1513. We sailed under the command of Juan Ponce De Leon for many days and nights to the coast of Florida, seeking the Fountain of Youth. He did not find it. But I did. I just did not know it at the time.

"In searching that land, I became lost and my thirst grew. I walked for a long time with no sight of my men or ship, looking desperately for water to drink. I found a rock. Water flowed from it to a big tree. At times, it would stop and start again. It was cool and tasted fresh, like new water from the sky. I then became sleepy and laid down my head to rest. When I woke up, I was able to return to my ship.

My commander asked me if I had located this Fountain of Youth. I told him 'no,' not realizing what I had found.

"In time, I got a job on land and met a woman. We were married. As time went on, she grew old but I did not. It was then that I realized what I had drank on that day in Florida.

"Eventually, my wife passed away as have all my children. Yet, I remain as young as before. They are still in my heart to this day but I know they can never come back to me.

"You know, Gunnar, once I met Christopher Columbus in Spain. He was trying to get money from the Queen and sailors like me so he could come here. If he could only see me now. I would tell him that I am not a sailor anymore. I work in computers. He would have no idea what I was talking about.

"But for about one hundred years, I was alone. Then I met Sherry. She remains the love of my life. No man has ever loved a woman like I love her. As long as I live, I could never love anyone like her again. She was my life, my love, my friend and my soul mate. She was just everything to me and God made her only for me. I know that now.

"I would go to a church once a year to light a candle and say a prayer for my first wife, Martha, and my children. I told them I would when they each died—to show my love would always be with them. I have kept my word to this day, Gunnar.

"But one year, in that church, I finished my prayer and turned and saw Sherry standing there like a little angel from heaven. I knew she was to become my second wife. That's how love is, Gunnar. It grabs you and it won't ever let you go—take my word on that.

"I had known her father for two years. I said to him, 'Samuel, you know I am a good man and a hard worker. Although today is the first day I have ever seen your daughter, I know I want her to be my wife. I don't have much, sir, but I can give her love until the day I die.'

"She was only sixteen, but she touched my heart in a way that no woman could after my Martha had died. I saw a woman in her that day and she had to be mine, no questions asked.

"Her father said to me, 'You can have her if you truly take care of her and love her. If you do not, you will be hearing from me, Pedro.'

"I did care for her and I still love her to this day.

"We were married that Sunday in that same church with her whole family there. But she never went back home with them that night. She

36

was mine from that day on. It felt so good to have a woman like her as my wife, sleeping with me in my bed, in my house. I can cry for the love I felt for my Sherry that night. It was that strong of a love. There are no words to express how I felt that day.

"But just to hear the name, Sherry, hurts me even now since I lost her so very long ago. Much time has passed without her by my side. I had true love, but no more. She was a part of me; a part of my soul.

"Before I met her, I had built a cabin in the forest. It was not a big place, but it was a good home for us to live in.

"After dinner, Sherry and I would go out for a walk over my land. We would hold hands and always stop by the river and just talk like a husband and wife do.

"We also had a vegetable garden, but it was flowers that she loved to grow. It always made her happy to see her flowers grow. One day as she tended to them, I saw Indians coming down the hill on their horses in war paint. I knew they had come to kill us. So I told Sherry to go into the house and lock herself in.

"I picked up some stones and put them in my pouch and watched the Indians come closer. I had no gun. All I needed were those stones and my slingshot against their bows and arrows.

"I stared them down. When I was a sailor, our cook always said, 'Come and get it if you want it!' I was thinking the same thing about those Indians. 'Here I am! Come and get it if you want it!'

"They launched their arrows at me. As if that would kill me.

"Wait," I say, "so this Fountain of Youth did more than just keep you young forever—it made you invincible?"

"Correct. Several arrows did strike me but I just pulled them out. Using stones from my sack, I hurled them with my slingshot. Hitting an Indian in the head, he would fall to the ground where I would run up to him with my knife and kill him and laugh about it. I was hit repeatedly, but every time I would just pull the arrows out and snap them in two. They could not believe their eyes.

"One of them charged me, throwing a knife from his horse. I was struck in the chest. That got me mad. I pulled it out and threw it back. He fell from his horse, dead. I just laughed at that damn Indian and the rest turned and ran away from me.

"I went back into the house and there was my sweet Sherry with tears in her eyes. I loved to look in those eyes. I kissed her and said, "Don't cry, my love. They can't kill me. Your love keeps me alive."

"She asked, 'Did they hurt you?' She was not able to find a mark, though the holes in my shirt told a very different story. 'You could have been killed out there. What would I do with you dead?'

"Some Indians thought I was a wild man. Some said I was a God. Others believed I was simply a man who could not die. And whenever I encountered them, they would just run away at the sight of me."

I say to him, "Seems kind of a shame to waste that kind of power planting vegetables."

"One time I went hunting for fresh meat—a deer or buffalo. I told Sherry I would return soon. Out on the prairie, I heard gunshots and went for a look. It was a covered wagon train being attacked by about a hundred wild Indians. I went to see if I could help somehow.

"The Indians saw me slip in. 'How are things going here?' I asked one man. He said, 'We need a doctor! My name is Finn, and I know it's dangerous out there but you know where town is, right?'

"I said to him, 'I'll get those Indians to turn around and go back home where they belong.' He thought I was crazy. I told him, 'Some Indians say I am crazy. I don't know if that's true or not, but they are frightened of me because of it. I'll show you.'

"I hopped on my horse and rode out with my rocks and sling shot. I fired them at the Indians on all four sides of the wagon train so they could all see me. I yelled, 'Come and get it! Fight with me and die by my hand!' They saw me and just turned and rode away.

"I returned to the wagon train and said to Finn, 'You see, they are frightened of me.'

"He said, 'I saw it with my own eyes but I still don't believe it.'

38

"I told him, 'Those Indians will not be back so long as they think I am still here with you nice people.'

"A woman gazed upon me with longing eyes. I smiled and said, 'You have beautiful eyes but I have my Sherry. You have the eyes but she has my heart. No one could ever take me away from her.

"I returned to Finn and said, 'Town is twenty-six miles that way. You should be there in two days if you are lucky. I need to get back before my wife thinks I've run off with another woman. So long.'

Eating pie, I say to Pedro, "I doubt the people in town were much better than those Indians, based on what I've seen of the Old West."

"True. There was a man who would intimidate people into buying him beer in this one bar. One day he tried it on me. I told him, 'Why, yes, coming right up! Bartender, can I have a beer, please?' I paid him and then I drank it.

"The man said, 'You drank my beer!'

"I said to him, 'I'm so sorry for that! Bartender, could I have other beer please?' I paid him and again I drank that beer, too.

"The man said to me, 'You think you're funny? You going to buy me my beer or not?'

"I said, 'Sure. Give me some money and I'll buy it for you.'

"He said, 'No, you buy my beer for me. You understand?'

"I told him, 'If I buy the beer, I will drink it. *You* understand?'

"The man said, 'You see my knife here?'

"I looked at it and said, 'Yes, what about it?'

"He said, 'If you don't buy my beer, I'll kill you with it right here in this bar.'

"I said to him, 'Well, if you're going to be like that, I will not buy you a beer and you can go to hell, big man.'

"The man stabbed his knife into my gut. I just pulled it out, looked at him and said, 'My turn' and let him have it. I saw the horror in his eyes as he looked at that blade go inside him and he fell to the floor, dead. I pulled it out of his body and went home."

I tell him, "You have a very special power, Pedro. My advice is that you make the best of it and live life to the fullest."

"Most men would do anything for this advantage I have. Yet, all I think of is my Sherry. I have had lots of wives and I loved them all. Sherry, though, she was different. The day she died my world came to an end. Nothing mattered to me—only my longing for her. What was there to live for without her in my life? If I could, I would say to God, 'Take me, but not my Sherry. She is a good person. I am a bad person. Take me instead of her, God.'

"As she got older, she told me it was okay to look at other women. She knew she would die soon and I would be alone again. She said, 'Just be happy. That is all I want for you. It will make me happy, too. I understand you are a man and need a woman. I'd love you anyway.'

"I said to her, 'No, Sherry, I love you more now than the day I first saw you. My heart has only grown. I do not see an old woman in bed; I just see the woman I love. I promised your father I would love you until the day I die. He is gone now but I've not broken my word. The body will die but love will live beyond death. Take my hand. You have my heart forever. You know that already. One day I will die but my love for you will go on with me to the place of lovers.'

"Sherry let go of my hand that day in our bed where we first made love on our wedding night. I kissed her one final time and I felt her spirit leave her body and go on to heaven.

"I looked around the house where we used to live. It felt so sad, cold and empty now that she was gone. I said, 'Sherry, you have my heart to keep. I cannot give it to anyone but you, my love. May God keep you for me, for one day we will be together again.'

"I cried all night long. My tears would not stop. I did not want to live without her love. I only wanted to die so I could be with her.

"The next day, I buried her by the flowers she planted. Little did she know they would mark her last place to sleep forever. I told her, 'Good-bye, my love. Until we meet again in Heaven.'

"With no escape, I turned to the bottle. Maybe it was the alcohol, but at times I would look to the sky and see her up there saying to me, 'Don't drink, Pedro; not for me.'

"So, Gunnar, I have lived a long time. But now, my love awaits. It is time for me to be with her again in heaven."

"I've heard your story, Pedro. How can I help you?"

"Gunnar, I want to go back in time before I drank that water so I can die like other people do. She and I can then be together right now in Heaven." He reaches for my arm and locks eyes with me. "You are the only one who can help me and you know it."

"I could do this for you, Pedro. However, realize that any children you had afterwards will not be born."

"I believe that God has a plan for everyone. I think that the water I drank was not a part of his plan, but was a curse instead. The souls of my children will be where God originally intended. I trust in that."

"All right, Pedro. Let's go."

I leave a tip on the table and we step out of the restaurant.

"See that big oak tree out there across the street?" I ask.

In front of the tree, I reach into my pocket and pull out a *revealer*, which looks like a couple of coins stacked on top of each other. I hand one to Pedro and have him put it in his pocket. "This device will keep you from freezing with the rest of the world when I activate my time machine." I then push my ring and ole Nelly materializes before us, ready to take us anywhere we want to go.

From the ground, she rises slowly and stops in the air. Her doors open and I tell Pedro, "Your long wait is over now. Let's get in."

He climbs in, looks around and says, "I am not ready to go back and die just yet, my friend. I would like to ask one more favor of you. Take me to see my sweet Sherry one more time before I say good-bye to this world and join her in Heaven. I want to see her in the church before we got married. That is where it all started for me—close to the water in Florida in1614."

"How could I say 'no' to you and your sweet Sherry?"

He gives me the exact place and time and I program the computer. We fire off into the past.

From what I can see, it's not really much of a town. Passing over the small church, I can see Pedro growing emotional.

We pass through its walls and hover inside. No one can see us.

Pedro goes numb and his eyes grow wide. "There she is. My love! I wish I could hold her in my arms one more time." He can only stare. "I just cannot bear to go. It is like leaving my heart there on that table. I would die without it just as surely as I have been dying without her. After all these years, this fire has not died out. Sherry, your last kiss is still with me. I still feel your lips next to mine."

I say to him, "I've seen lots of men and women together but I've never seen a love like yours. The way you to talk of her—"

"No, it is not the way I talk of her, it is my heart that talks of her. I do not know how to talk to women. Only my heart can talk for me. And it was not I that first saw Sherry; it was my heart that saw her there and it knew her heart, too, and knew we could be happy together forever. It said to me, 'Get up and go to my love, Pedro, right now or I will stop your heart right here and now and you will die without this love of your life."

I ask, "Can anybody find true love like you and Sherry had?"

"Yes, it is easy, he said. Just let your heart find it for you. Do not look on the outside of a woman. One's eyes are blind. Look with your heart's eyes. That will tell you if she is the only one for you. There, you will find the true love you are looking for."

"Pedro, you really lucked out. She is very beautiful and even has good manners. You love her *and* she loves you."

Pedro says, "And there she is, right in front of me, smiling like an angel. I would give anything to have her in my arms and kiss her one more time. But this cannot be. Her father would kill me anyway if he saw me with his unmarred daughter."

"Pedro, do you have five cents on you?"

"Um, yes."

42

"Can I have it please?"

He goes into his pocket and gives it to me.

"Thanks. Now you can hold and kiss your sweet Sherry."

I open the door and everyone stops moving. We get out and he walks slowly to her. He stares a moment before dropping to his knees. I have never seen a man cry like this for a woman.

He says to her, "I love you more than you will ever know. For all these years, you were in my heart. It has never died. Please look at me with your beautiful eyes."

If I had given him the revealer to give her, she could move again. But in this time, she does not know him. Her reaction would break his heart. I will not say anything about it to him. Although it hurts me to see this man so in love with this woman here, it has to be this way.

He holds her hand and kisses it softy. "I love you, Sherry. I love you so much."

He gets up, still crying for this woman he cannot have. He holds her hand and kisses it one more time. Looking at her, he does not kiss her lips, but only her forehead and says, "Good-bye, my love. I will go to die for our love now, so we will be together again."

"Let us leave, Gunnar. My heart cannot take any more of this."

We head back inside the time machine. Pedro sees Sherry moving and talking again. He sees that she is happy. "It is time for me to go, Gunnar. Death is waiting for me."

We leave the church and make our way to the time and place he drank from the Fountain of Youth. We do not speak a word until we get there. "It is over here, Gunnar." We walk to the spot, cover it up so no one could find it again and then go back inside.

Eventually, we see Pedro walking past the water without seeing it.

There is a bright, white flash.

I felt disoriented for a moment, as I find myself in the restaurant giving my order to the waiter.

I usually see someone else here to talk to. But not today.

I eat my pie, pay the man and walk home.

Chapter 6: **Ransom**

Lying in bed, my phone rings and wakes me up. I answer it. "Hello?"

"Gunnar, it's Debbie. Can you come to the FBI office right now?"

"You okay?"

"Fine. I need to see you right away. I'm in Charles Lewis' office."

"I'll be there in fifteen minutes."

I go downstairs and out to the backyard where my time machine is parked. I press onto my ring and she instantly appears, looking at me like she's ready to go. I climb inside and say, "Let's go, Nelly. I have a feeling Debbie needs our help real bad."

I fly across the bay to San Francisco and park outside the Federal Bureau of Investigation building and hurry inside.

I find Debbie in Agent Lewis' office.

"So what's up?"

Debbie says, "Come in and shut the door, please. I'm glad you got here so quickly."

Agent Lewis sits behind a large oak desk. "Have a seat, Mr. Best. This isn't easy for me. I know I gave my word to you and to Agent Alley's former superior that I would not ask about your time machine that brought her here from 1956. But today I must break my word to you and to my dear friend."

I quickly stand. "I knew people like you can't keep your word. It's my machine and you can't have it! I'm going to get a beer."

"Gunnar!" Debbie shouts, "You will sit down right now and listen to Agent Lewis! You hear me?"

I slowly lower myself into my seat.

"Go head," she says to him.

"I think Doug Marcus would understand my position. But if you choose not to help, I'll understand and Debbie will still have a job."

"Tell me what happened."

"Gunnar, a girl has been taken. The kidnapers want money or they say they'll kill her if their demands are not met. Her mother has asked me for my help. Frankly, I'm at a loss here.

"I want you to hear this." He activates a tape recorder on his desk.

"We have your daughter, Mr. Jacob, and we want one-hundred-thousand dollars or she's dead. You understand?"

"What's your name?" a frightened man asks. "And how do I know you really have my daughter?"

"My name is John Smith. You want proof? I will give you proof. Which finger do you want cut off and mailed to you? Or do you want her whole hand instead? That's a good deal because you'll get all her fingers back instead of just one."

"No, Mr. Smith. I'll take your word."

"Tomorrow at twelve o'clock—high noon—take the money to the grocery store by your home and have your cell phone with you at all times. Remember, your daughter's life is on the line here."

Agent Lewis stops the tape player. "The next day, Mr. Jacob went to the store with the FBI monitoring him. His cell phone rang and the kidnapper ordered him to go to customer service. He was told to have them wire the money, which they did. The kidnappers said they would release the girl after they had withdrawn the funds. He also told him to say 'hi' to the FBI. That was two days ago."

"What some people will do for money…" Debbie comments.

"So," Agent Lewis says, "I thought if your time machine could go back in time, we could follow her and the people who took her."

Debbie says to me, "I told him that it's not mine to use. It belongs to you, Gunnar. If it were mine, I'd use it to save that girl right now. I said you could help if you wanted, but he needed to talk to you."

"The truth is," Agent Lewis says, "the mother of the kidnapped girl is my sister. Her daughter, Janet, is my niece. If she's hurt in any way, I just don't know how we could live with that. I can't make you do this because I'm Agent Alley's boss. But I feel like my hands are tied here—like there's nothing more I can do. I've got every available

46

agent looking for her right now but she's gone. I know you can find her with your time machine if you wanted to."

"Agent Lewis," I inquire, "If this little girl was not your sister's daughter, would you have called me to help?"

"I'm not going to lie to you, Gunnar. Probably not. Does it make you any happier to hear that?"

"It's a lot different when it's not your own family," I say to him. "I respect you for telling me the truth. I'll help you with Janet and I'm sorry for the way I spoke before. Sometimes I react without thinking. I hope you understand."

"Thanks, Gunnar. Let's do what we can to get her back home."

"One thing first. My name must never be mentioned in connection to Janet or Debbie or a time machine. People have a way of breaking their word of silence. Right, Agent Lewis?"

He nods with a guilty face.

"If I am betrayed, I'll have no choice but to take Janet back to her kidnappers and this talk will never have happened. Are we clear?"

"I will do as you say."

"Now, tell me where she lives."

He jots down her address and hands me her picture.

"Pretty girl," I mention.

"May I come?" he asks. "If you need help, I'll be right there."

"No, Charles, I can do this myself. But I thank you anyway. When I come back, though, you owe me a case of beer."

"Anything you want, you got it."

"Debbie, I'll be a little late for dinner. Tell my brother I had to do a job for the FBI." I turn to Lewis with a smirk. "They couldn't do it themselves and had to call in the best. Gunner Best that is. Ha, ha!"

I go outside and press my ring. My powerful craft slowly rises and stops mid-air as its doors open for me.

I step in and say, "Nelly, we have a job to do. There's no money in it, as usual, but there is a young girl that needs our help."

I program the dashboard computer to take us back to Janet's home two days ago and launch us on our way.

Soon enough, I see her coming out of her house. She's wearing a white dress and coat. She's a little older than she looks in her picture. I'd say about sixteen.

I follow her in my time machine all the way to school.

She sees a young man and calls his name. "Rick!"

He sees her but is with another young pretty girl to whom he says, "See you later, okay? Love you, Sarah." He discreetly pats her bottom but Janet does not see this. He's about twenty-five and good-looking. Smoking a cigarette, he's in a light blue shirt with brown pants.

He walks over to Janet and whispers, "Give me a kiss."

She replies, "Okay, but people are looking."

They kiss anyway and he says, "Let's go back to my place."

They walk to an old apartment building and go in. I follow them. Going through walls in my time machine is like cutting through butter with a hot knife and it does so without a sound.

Climbing up the stairs, he says, "I'm so glad you decided to come and live with me, Janet. I love you so much. I'm going to make you so happy. You'll see.

"You did turn off your cell phone, right?"

"Yeah, I did what you told me to do," she responds.

"Good. Your parents may not be too happy with your decision and won't stop calling for a while. We don't need that right now. In fact, why don't you give me your phone to make it easier on you."

Hesitantly, she hands the phone over to him.

They enter a small apartment and settle onto a sofa.

"Janet, have you ever made love? Tell the truth. Our love means so much and I want to be the only one in your life from now on."

"I've never had sex with anyone if that's what you want to know."

"Janet, I love you. You know that. Now that you're living here with me, I'd like to be totally honest with you about something. I have

48

a heart problem but have no money now. If I don't buy my medicine, I'll die. I don't know what to do."

I'm sitting in ole Nelly listening to this, but I don't believe a damn word I'm hearing.

Janet asks, "Is there anything I can do? We can go to my father. He has a lot of money."

"I don't want his help." An idea seems to come to him. "But you know what… maybe there is a way you can help after all. No, I can't. It would be wrong of me to say anything like this to you, my love."

"Just tell me, Rick," Janet begs.

"Please don't make me say it. I'd rather die young and in love."

"Please Rick, tell me!"

"Okay, but only because you really want to hear it. I know a man who has a lot of money. He told me once he would give a thousand dollars to make love with a young girl. It meant nothing to me at the time and I certainly never thought of you—believe me, because I love you so much. But when you just asked me how you could help, that thought did come to me."

"Well, what would I have to do for him?"

"Whatever he wants. Only then will he give us the money we need and we can live together and be happy together forever."

"I don't know. I don't love him or even know this guy."

"How strong is your love for me? Just tell me. I can take it. Does it really matter to you if I die?"

"You know me better than that Rick!"

"If you truly love someone, sometimes you got to make sacrifices for them. I've never asked you for anything before, have I?"

Janet stops and thinks for a moment, appearing very conflicted.

"Well, will you do it for me?"

Reluctantly, she replies, "Okay."

"Remember, though, you will do anything he wants. I can't break my word to him."

"I won't know what I'm doing, but I'll try."

"Thank you, Janet! You just saved my life. I'll pay you back for this somehow, someday. Wait and see. I'll go talk to him right now. Is it okay if he comes over today? I need my medicine now."

"Let's just get it over with."

"First, we'll need to take some pictures so he can see what he's getting for his money."

"Do we have to?"

"Please, Janet. If you were buying a dress, wouldn't you like to see it first before you bought it?"

"I guess so."

"Good. Now take off your clothes."

"What?"

"What's the problem? You're taking your clothes off for him later anyway. Did you think you were having sex with your clothes on?"

"But what if someone else sees them?"

"You have my word that no one else ever will. It's the only way we can get the money for my medicine. So what will it be? Picture or no picture? Will I live or die? My life's in your hands, Janet."

Janet sighs and starts unbuttoning her blouse.

"Let me do that for you," Rick quickly says. "I have never taken a woman's clothes off before."

Here I am, watching this creep strip the clothes off of this sixteen-year-old child. I may just kill Rick for what he's making her do. But I must wait until the time is right to make my move.

"Nice. Now come with me. My camera is in the bedroom."

She's obviously very insecure about this whole thing but still goes along with him. Why, I don't know.

"Could you lay on the bed for me, sweetie? I think it would look very sexy for the photo."

She does so and he starts taking many pictures of her.

"Seeing you in bed—naked like that—you will never know how much I want you right now. Momma mia! I want you so bad it hurts."

50

Staring at this sixteen-year-old girl's naked body in bed, he can't take it anymore. He takes off his shirt and pants, leaving his shorts on. He lies on top of her and kisses all over her young body, touching her breasts with his dirty hands.

I watch, growing sickened.

As he bites and kisses her breasts, he says to her, "I'd give almost anything to have you now." He sighs and puts his clothes back on. "I got to go meet this guy. You should take a shower before he comes and get all prettied up. I know he'll like you very much."

He grabs his coat and says, "Remember to do whatever he wants. Make him happy and you'll make me happy."

He walks out the door and locks it.

What's wrong with this girl? Can't she see what this guy is doing?

I feel like getting her out right now but I can't. It's not time yet. What a shame to see such a young girl in love go through this. I'll be back for you young lady and you can count on it.

I follow Rick. He gets into a car and drives to a bar south of town. He goes in and approaches a man in a brown jacket and black pants. His yellow shirt is patterned with flowers which barely contains his three-hundred pounds of fat.

I move in close so I can hear every word.

"Hello there, Fred. I have good news for you—something you'll like—a nice piece of ass if you want it."

"Rick, I always like a nice piece of ass, especially young ass. And you're always good at getting it for me. That's what I like about you. What do you have for me today? I hope she's young and pretty—the way I like 'em."

"She's only sixteen and she's smoking hot. I know you'll love her. I got pictures. You tell me, who wouldn't like this young thing?"

Rick shows Fred the images on an old laptop.

"Let me see what you got there. Ah... I can look at stuff like this all day long."

Fred stares at her pictures with lust in his eyes, studying every line of Janet's young, naked body.

"Sometimes I wonder where you get all these pretty girls for me."

"It's not that hard. You just got to know how to talk to them. Most girls are real dumb. They're just lacking in common sense and will do anything for you if you tell them you love them—even have sex with somebody else they don't know. I just love the stupid ones."

Another man comes in, walks up to Fred and states, "Here's that three-hundred I owe you on the horses."

Fred takes a little book out from his coat. He opens it and marks something on one of its pages. Putting it back into his pocket, he says, "Play the horses and pay me. I like that, don't you?"

As the man turns and walks away, another man approaches and throws down a one-hundred dollar bill. Fred looks into his little book and tells him, "You owe me two-hundred more, asshole. Do you see that clock on the wall?"

"Yeah," the man replies. "So what?"

"When the big hand and little hand hit 'twelve,' that's tomorrow. You will be in a lot of pain if I don't get my money then. Understand? You play the horses and lose, you have to pay me. Now get the hell out of here. You know what I do to people who don't pay up."

The man turns and leaves with a look of intimidation on his face.

"This is nice, Rick. Real nice. I like this picture of her. So young and sweet. I can almost taste her. Just look at those legs and breasts. They taste so good with a little whip cream. You should try it."

Rick replies, "I have!"

She looks like a little child in this picture. So young and innocent, like she could do no wrong.

Rick asks, "How come you never got no girlfriend with you?"

"Well, I'll tell you the truth. You take a woman out to a nice place to eat and have some drinks. You then take her back to her place and she'll say 'It was fun,' but she will also say 'goodnight and that's it.' With these girls, you don't have to take them out anywhere and talk about stupid things you don't give a damn about when in the back of your mind, you're only really thinking about getting laid. Screw that. You can even beat these girls for the fun of it and tell them to do any sex act the way you like and she'll do it. It's better this way. This bar is mine and I own apartments. I got money and get all the sex I want. What would I want a girlfriend for?"

"And you can be the first to touch the soft skin and kiss those red lips of this little angel if you want to."

"How much you want for her?"

"Since I like you, how about a thousand? It's a good deal and you know it, too. This sixteen-year-old said she'd let you do anything you want for as long as you want it. Otherwise, I know someone else who will give me twelve for her. He'll have a good time with her instead."

"She'll do anything for me, you say?"

"Anything. You name it and she'll do it for you."

"Even if I want to tie her up and whip her with my belt? I like to see little girls cry out then kiss 'em where I just hit 'em. I say, 'Does that help stop the pain?' It's better than sex—although I do that, too."

"Sounds okay with me. You are paying for it and I like to keep my customers happy. Just cover her mouth or the neighbors might talk."

"The last young one I had was Betty. Remember her?"

"Your other friend got her for you, but yeah, I remember."

"She was fifteen—another runaway. Her parents were mean to her so she came to my house because I was good to her with my belt!" Fred laughs. "If her parents were so mean, why did she cry out for her mother so much? I would go to sleep so tired after her, but so happy.

"My friend, Eric, would go out for 'em like a wild animal looking for prey. Bus stops are the best. You know that don't you? Girls there are looking around with nowhere to go and no one waiting for them. She'd be all alone, not knowing what she's going to do out in this big world; her first time away from home. So Eric would talk to her, buy her food and become her friend. He'd tell her that a man—me—will give her a job cleaning his house and a place to stay."

"I should be writing this down!" Rick remarks.

"He'd bring her over to my house and I'd say, 'You got the job. Let me show you your room.' Then we'd close the door and she's got nowhere to go. She's ours to do whatever we please. So we'd tie her up and cut her clothes off and flip a coin to see who gets her first. I'd always call heads and he'd say, 'Let the best man win.'

"The next day, we might sell her to someone else. That's life and it's easy money for us."

"Sounds like a sweet deal."

"But those parties we used to have at my house in the country— out in the middle of nowhere—no one could hear anything, says Fred. I'd have Betty or some other girl tied in the back room in that big bed where I kept my women. All my friends would have their way with her. You could hear her screaming so loud.

"One guy would talk to her like she was his wife! He'd say, 'I'm tired of you telling me what to do,' and smack her in the face. He was pretty sick but he had a lot of money so we let him.

"Occasionally, a guy would bring his son over to have sex for the first time. It worked out pretty good for the boys because the girl was their age and she was always real pretty. They could do anything they wanted and she couldn't say 'no.' There was no stopping them!"

"I know! I was one of them!"

"That's right!"

They both laugh out loud.

"Whatever happened to her?" Rick asks. "She was good."

"She was, but I sold her for a couple thousand to a friend. He says she still brings in the money or he lets her have it. I think she likes to get hit in the face."

These guys are a real piece of work.

"Rick, if this girl of yours is as good as I think she is and makes me happy today, would you be willing to sell her? I sold my last one because she got too old. She got to be twenty."

"Sure, but it's going to cost you two thousand cash. No returns."

"Sounds like a good enough deal to me."

"But if you do buy her, can I ask you a favor?"

"What is it?"

"Can I have her once? She looked so good in that bed of mine."

"Yeah, you can have her anytime you want. Hell, when I'm done, all of my friends can have her anytime they want, too. That's just the generous kind of man I am."

"You got a deal, Fred. At first, I just wanted her a week or two for myself, but then it occurred to me she was a virgin and I could get me a lot more money with that body of hers. I could then buy someone else and have money left over."

Fred passes Rick a stack of cash under a napkin.

He then stares at her picture again. "I'm going to have some fun with her. She may not have fun with me but who cares.

"Oh, and don't come home until I'm done. You hear?"

"No problem."

"Rick, thank you for seeing me first."

"You bet," he says with a grin.

Fred gets up and walks out to have his way with Janet. But it will not happen—not if I have anything to say about it. Ole Nelly is faster than any car on this world.

Almost instantly, I'm back at the apartment. Out in the hall, I get out and retrieve some ropes and cloth from the rear compartment. The time machine vanishes and I go to the door and knock.

"Who is it?"

"Janet, I think you know why I'm here. Rick sent me."

She pauses. "Okay wait a minute."

"But I don't want you to see my face. So when you open the door, keep your eyes closed. Rick said you'd do as I say."

"I know." I hear the door being unlocked. "My eyes are closed."

I enter and look around. She has a white dress on and looks like a sweet angel. I take my rope and say, "Turn around and put your hands behind your back so I can tie you up. Is that okay with you, Janet?"

"It's okay with me, mister, if it makes you happy." A tear escapes, although she's trying not to cry. "I think you should know, I've never had sex before."

"I know. Rick told me."

"Mister, what's your name? You don't have to say your last name. Just your first name."

"Why do you want to know?"

"I'd like to know the name of the first man I have sex with."

"It's better that you just call me 'mister.' You'll see why later."

As I tie her hands she asks, "Mister, do you have a girlfriend?"

"Not exactly. Why do you ask?"

"We are going to have sex and I would like to know if you are a good person or a bad person."

"Janet, you'll find out in time what kind of man I am."

With her hands tied up, I tell her, "Now I'll be covering your eyes. Is that okay with you?"

"Rick told me to do whatever you want with me. So do whatever you want with me."

As I prepare her blindfold she says, "Next week is my birthday. I will be seventeen. I've never even been kissed before—that's not true. I did kiss Rick today. He is my boyfriend and I love him very much. That's why I'm letting you do this to me. Because of him."

"Happy birthday."

"Thank you."

I put on her blindfold.

"Mister, are you going to hurt me? I hear men like to see women in a lot of pain. Is that why you tied my hands up like an animal and won't let me see your face? Will you cover my mouth next or do you like to hear a woman scream when you torture her in bed?"

"That's not why I came here. Take my word for it and don't cry. I know it's scary not knowing what'll happen to you next, but I don't like it when a woman starts to cry in front of me. It bothers me."

She breaks down even more. "I'm not even a woman! Not yet. I just want to go back home to my mother."

"You promised Rick—right?"

"I'm sorry, sir. Don't tell Rick. I'll be good, I promise."

"I'll have to cover your mouth now."

Sobbing, she says, "I won't try to cry out."

I take another cloth and wrap it around her mouth and then tie her legs together so she cannot move.

I place a revealer in her pocket and push down on my ring. I open the apartment door and find my time machine outside waiting for me.

"Janet, I'm not who you think I am. I'm working for your uncle at the FBI and you're coming with me back home."

She pauses and tries to squirm away. I pick her up and put her in my time machine and close the door.

"I know you're angry with me now but before this day is over, you'll be thanking me. Don't forget I said that to you."

I program Nelly to take us back to when Rick had met with Fred.

With her eyes and mouth still covered, I say to her, "Listen."

Rick enters and greets Fred. Over the next few minutes, she grows shocked by what they say about her and the other girls taken.

Fred boasts to Rick, "Even if I want to tie her up and whip her with my belt? I like to see little girls cry out then kiss 'em where I just hit 'em. I say, 'Does that help stop the pain?' It's better than sex—although I do that, too."

"Sounds okay with me. You are paying for it and I like to keep my customers happy. Just cover her mouth or the neighbors might talk."

Janet begins to weep.

"Rick, if this girl of yours is as good as I think she is and makes me happy today, would you be willing to sell her? I sold my last one because she got too old. She got to be twenty."

"Sure, but it's going to cost you two thousand cash. No returns."

Janet shakes her head, unable to listen to anymore.

"Heard enough?" I ask.

57

She nods.

"If I take that off your mouth, will you stay quiet and be good to me?—I don't mean that sexually—just be good."

She nods again and I remove her gag.

"Thank you," she says. "Damn you, though. But I still thank you." She breaks down in tears again. "I can't believe it. He thinks I'm just property. I can't even imagine the suffering you saved me from."

"We should go now."

I take her to the Federal Building—two days into the future—and park near Agent Lewis's office.

Janet says, "I'll give you my virginity if you want it. It's all I can think of to repay you right now."

"You're a bit young for me, but thanks anyway."

I take the revealer from her pocket and she suddenly looks more like a board than a person. I then lug her out.

Agent Lewis sits frozen behind his big desk. I place Janet within a chair and take off her ropes. I then go back into my time machine and close the doors. The timeline resumes. Hidden from their view, I see Agent Lewis noticing Janet in front of him.

Quickly, he goes to her and removes her blindfold.

"How did I get here?" she asks.

Agent Lewis replies, "I don't care. I'm just glad you're safe."

Debbie enters to see what is going on. Since she keeps a revealer with her at all times, she can see me in my time machine but does not say anything about it.

Agent Lewis asks, "What happened to you?"

Janet starts to cry. "I made a huge mistake. I went with this guy, Rick. I thought he loved me but I was wrong. He just wanted to use me for money. But there was another man—a good man—and he only wanted to get me out of there. He didn't give his name but said he worked for the FBI. Is that true? Does he work here, Uncle Charles?"

"I don't know the man you're talking about."

At this point, I decide to park Nelly outside and then walk back into the federal building.

As I enter Agent Lewis' office, he says to me, "Oh! Thank you for coming back. You know what I mean."

"And who is this?" I ask with a scratchy voice. "Sorry, I seem to have developed a slight cold."

"Gunnar, this is my niece, Janet."

"Nice to meet you, Janet. You're a pretty young lady.

"Thank you."

She steps to the window and looks out.

I say to him, "I just stopped by for that beer money you owe me. You remember, don't you?"

"Of course."

Janet abruptly turns. "It's you! You're the one who saved me. I'd know your voice anywhere."

She runs up and gives me a big kiss on the lips.

Debbie does not know how to react.

"Young lady, you have me confused with someone else. This past hour I was across the street drinking beer—until I ran out of money."

"But it is you. You're my hero! Don't deny it. You know it and I know it, too."

"I've been called a lot of things in my time, but never a hero."

"It's just—your voice—it sounds so much like his voice."

"How much money do you need?" Charles asks.

"Twenty should do it." He hands me the cash. "Thanks. So long for now. And thanks for the kiss, Janet. It was good."

I step out but wait to hear what Janet says next.

"Who was he?" I hear her ask.

Charles responds, "A good friend of ours. And if he asked me for a hundred or five-hundred dollars, I'd give it to him.

"I'm going to call your parents now."

I step away. At the elevator, Debbie runs up to me.

"What about the kidnappers?" she asks.

I hand her a piece of paper. "Here's all the info you need on them. Not sure who got the idea about a kidnapping. They must've come up with that at some point in the last two days since I left them. I trust you to figure it all out for yourself. You'll also find them connected with a number of other missing girls."

"Thank you, Gunnar." She kisses me on the cheek.

Chapter 7: **Target Practice**

After a few beers at the nice bar across the street from the Federal Building, I strike up a conversation with the bartender.

"Did you know there are people out there on other worlds in outer space? Did you ever see a Gettion? They have big heads and big eyes and a small mouth and are very shiny. If you ever see one, you must kill them or they will try to kill you."

"If you say so. Another beer, sir?"

"Yes, please."

While drinking it, I begin thinking about the first time Jack—who I inherited my time machine from—showed me how to use a gun. It was 1714 in Tombstone, Arizona. Well, it was before the town had been established, but in the same spot. I think I'll go back there again.

I go out, look about and push on my ring. There, my time machine appears before for me. Its doors begin to open and I go in. I sit down within my cushy bucket seat and say, "Come on, Nelly, let's go. I got a job for you, old girl." I program the controls for 1714 and up we go.

In a flash, we arrive at what would be Tombstone in Arizona.

This place is good because it has a lot of rocks all around.

"Show me what you got, Nelly. I want to see."

We ascend high up in the air. While in a hover, I fire a laser shot, which splits a large rock in half. "Pretty nice, ole girl."

I shoot at some more and keep it up for a while, firing the lasers again and again. I feel like I'm getting better.

Now it's time to try a laser-guided bomb. With it, I explode a very large boulder. Wow, that does a nice job!

Now I'll practice flying and firing at the same time. Let's see if I can hit those rocks there. I move in and shoot but miss completely.

I swing around for another pass but I miss again.

Maybe I better go slower this time.

That did the trick. Nailed it.

Now I'll go a bit faster. Damn it! Missed again! I must keep doing this until I can hit it cleanly. It's harder than you might think.

Those rocks must be moving on me. That must be it. How else can I miss? After all, I'm a good shot and I am from Texas. Sounds like a good excuse anyway. "Rock, don't move anymore. You hear? That's a good rock, now."

I try again and this time I strike it! "Good rock! Thank you, rock! Tombstone, I owe you one rock."

Now I go a bit faster and still hit my target. I try it even faster and hit it again and again.

My skill with the laser-guided bombs is getting better, too. Over and over, I hit whatever I'm aiming for. Damn, I'm good.

As fun as this is, I know it's much more terrifying when in battle. John, from the time planet, Antonion, warned me of the alien race, the Gettion, I spoke of earlier. I encountered them once before and was nearly taken out. They see us only as animals to experiment on.

The next time I see those alien bastards, I'll be ready for them.

Now, though, it's time to go back home.

Arriving at my house, I see a strange car parked out front.

I gently set my time machine down, and as its doors open for me, I get out and walk into the house.

I discover Larry, my astronaut friend, in the living room drinking coffee with my brother. He sees me and stands up as I enter. I wonder what's on his mind. I'll bet he wants something.

Shaking my hand, he says "Hi, Gunnar. How you doing out here in California?"

"All the girls like me out here and I like them, too, as you know. What's up, Larry? What brings you to our neck of the woods?"

"Well, Gunnar, nobody knows where Ed is. I called all his friends but nobody knows a damn thing. So I phoned up Jim, who introduced you to us, and he told me to look you up. You know were Ed's at?"

I chuckle. "Yeah, I do. And I'll tell you this: nobody will ever find him here on this planet. That's for sure."

"What do you mean by that?"

"Remember back in that bar in Florida, I told you about this other world where aliens live, and that they were my friends?"

"Yeah..."

"Well, I took Ed there and he liked it so much, he decided to stay. He's very happy and likes the women too much."

"That's Ed for you," Larry says. "But can you do me a big favor? There's beer in it for you."

"How many beers are we talking here?"

"All the beer you can drink. How does that sound, old buddy?"

"I know what you want, Larry. You want me to take you to Ed. You know I only have one extra seat. If you both come back with me, who's going to sit on who's lap? Can you tell me that?"

"Let's cross that bridge if we come to it."

"Ed's happy where he is. Just let him be with his new friends."

"Please, Gunnar, can you just do this favor for me?"

"I should say 'no' but you are my friend, too. All right. I've got to get some sleep first, though. It's a long trip ahead of us. We can leave at five a.m. That okay with you?"

"That would be great. I'll see you in the morning, then."

I ask my brother James, "Can you show Larry to the guestroom?"

"No problem."

"Good-night," I tell them.

Come morning, Larry is already up. "I see you're all packed and ready to go," I tell him. "That coffee looks good."

As I sip my cup, Larry asks, "What happened with that lady from the museum I saw you with in Florida? What was her name? Emily? How was it with her? Ever get lucky?"

"Nope. Long story. One day I might tell you about it. Although, if I did get lucky, I wouldn't tell you about it anyway."

He grins.

"This coffee is good, but it's time. Let's go," I say.

As we go outside, I ask Larry, "You still have your revealer?"

"You mean that thingy that looks like two coins stuck together?" He takes it out of his pocket and shows me.

"Yep, that's the one. Now turn around."

He does so and I press on my ring. The time machine materializes and rises a little off the ground as a shimmer of color dances over its gleaming surface. The doors start to open. We walk over them to get in and the doors close behind us after we are seated. I pull back on the steering wheel and the mighty craft ascends up to the heavens. Once clear of the Earth's atmosphere, I press the preprogrammed button to take us to the planet, Antonion.

You know, Gunnar, as an astronaut I have seen a few spaceships in my day, but I have to say I like yours the best. I feel like a human being inside here and not like another machine."

"Yeah, I love my baby."

After flying a while, I pull out my conductor to call John.

"What's that?" Larry asks.

"It's called a 'conductor.' It works like a cell phone but can also transport your entire body to any address you choose."

"Why can't we just use it to get there now?"

"It needs the satellites stationed over the planet we're going to. I can still use it as a phone, though, to call ahead."

I punch in John's number and wait for him to pick up. "Hey, John, this is Gunnar!"

"Greetings, Gunnar! What can I do for you?"

"Just wanted to let you know I'll be swinging by very soon with another friend of mine from Earth."

"It will be good to see you again."

"Likewise. Can you give me Ed's number so I can call him?"

"Sure, hang on." After giving it to me, I thank him and hang up.

"He sure speaks good English," Larry comments.

"Oh, there's a computer that translates. There's more technology on their planet to assist with that, too."

"I see."

64

I'm sure he has no idea what the heck I'm talking about. People just say they do even when they don't.

"Let's give ole Ed a call, shall we?" I suggest. I punch his number into my conductor. "Hi, Ed! It's Gunnar."

"Gunner! Thanks so much again for bringing me to this world. I'll never know how to thank you!"

"Ed, I've got someone here who wants to talk to you." I hand the phone to Larry.

"Hi, Ed!" he says, "How's that new planet been treating you?"

"Larry!" he shouts. "It's great out here! I've got a fantastic place. It's actually Gunnar's but he lets me stay rent-free. How about that! What've you been up to?"

"I've been missing my old friend, big guy. You know it's costing me a fortune in beer to pay Gunnar to come out here to see you."

"You're coming to visit?"

"We're on our way right now."

"Woot!" Larry yells.

"I hear you have a girlfriend," says Ed.

"I love all the women out here. Gunnar will tell you why. I don't really have a girlfriend because I'm from Earth. Chicks here love that! I'm a hot deal on this world."

"I'm sure. We'll see you in a little while. So long, Ed."

"Cheers."

Larry hands me the conductor. "Thanks again for taking me."

"It's okay. I might just get lucky there again. We'll be there soon. You'll see fire outside the window. Should look familiar to you when we enter the atmosphere."

Larry looks out and says, "It's so beautiful out here. There are no words to express what I'm seeing out here in this new solar system. The stars aren't like the ones back home, you know that?"

"Well, we are very far away. Ole Nelly here is going very fast."

"I can see why Ed would want to come out here. I can't believe my eyes! It would be impossible to explain in words to anyone who has not seen it for themselves—and I'm an astronaut!"

We are now approaching Antonion.

Entering the atmosphere, the time machine's skin glows red-hot. But she can take a lot of heat. "Easy does it, Nelly. Come on, baby. Show Larry what you got in you."

Safely, we settle to the ground and then slowly rise a few inches. The doors open and we climb out.

"Welcome to Antonion, Larry; where the beer is always cold and the women are always hot. What you do on this planet is up to you. Neither me or Ed won't say anything to your wife or anyone else."

"I don't think that'll be necessary."

"Think about it. Women here can't betray you because they live on another planet. They don't have your number, and even if they did, a call will not get to our planet so you're safe any way you look at it."

"I suppose."

"Maybe have some fun, then. You're a big boy now. You can do anything you want out here."

"You saw my wife. She's beautiful, too. I couldn't do anything to hurt her. You could have the most beautiful woman in the world in front of me and I'd still say 'no' because there is no woman better."

"Well, I know you're a good man and I know you love your wife; but just in case, know that we won't tell."

"Thanks, but no woman could get in the way of how I feel."

"Okay, let's go to my place and see Ed." I take out my conductor and say to Larry, "Give me your hand."

He gives me a funny look. "Excuse me?"

"You heard me. It's the fastest way to get there. Otherwise, it's a long walk. What'll it be?"

Larry gives me his hand and says, "No kissing, understand?"

"There's no way you'll ever get one of my kisses, Larry."

66

With his hand firmly in mine, I press on my conductor. A second later, we're at my apartment.

I knock on my door. Ed answers with a pretty girl beside him.

"Hey!" he shouts. He gives Ed and me enthusiastic hugs.

Blanca—my favorite lady here on Antonion—comes to the door. She looks so hot standing there all dressed up with her beautiful body and those beautiful eyes. She knows how to dress so a man will look at her and I do like to look up and down at her.

"Hello, Blanca," I say.

"Ed told me you were coming back," she responds. "He asked if I wanted to come over for a party in your honor."

I peer into the apartment. "Party?"

"I told him I would love to come and see you again."

Ed says, "Come on in and join the fun!"

Larry and I enter and see lots of smiling people.

Ed directs my attention to the woman by his side. "You remember Sarah—Blanca's friend? She's the one who came to the bar that day we first got here."

"Of course. Hi, Sarah. It's nice to see you again. You look just as pretty as the last time I saw you."

"Hello, Gunnar. You still look good to me, too, Earthman."

"And you know Claudia," Larry continues. "We met her at that Western bar the last time you were here."

"Yes, she is not someone who is easily forgotten."

What beautiful eyes and what a body!

"How's Earth?" she asks.

"It's nice. One day you should go. I know you'd like it. Speaking of which, this is Larry. He's a good friend of mine and Ed."

"Hi, Earthman. Welcome to my world. Do you come in peace?"

Larry replies, "Yes, I do. You are the first to call me "Earthman." I like it coming from you."

Larry discreetly looks her over; especially at her low-cut blouse. I can tell he likes what he sees.

"Let us sit down there and talk," Claudia suggests. "I would like to know everything about Earth. Your people seem so nice to talk to."

Larry tries to stay calm as they go to the couch. I can't help but listen in. "You know, Larry, men on this planet don't know the right way to talk to a woman or treat them. But I know men from Earth do. Our men just think of themselves. I see how Gunnar treats Blanca and the way Ed treats Sarah and I like it."

Larry is unsure of how to respond.

"Do you think I am pretty?"

"I think you're pretty to anyone who sees you, without question."

She is very beautiful. Just look at that body. God stopped making women like that a long time ago and no telling if he will make another like her again. Twice she offered herself to me, but I was with Blanca. It's hard to say "no" to a woman who looks like that. I'm only human. She said she wanted an Earthman and asked if I would take her to my world as my woman there. I still think of her as the one that got away.

"You know, Larry," she says, "when I was a girl, other girls made fun of me because of my large breasts. It hurt me and made me cry. But you like my breasts, don't you, Larry?"

"Um, yes, I do. They're very beautiful to look at from here."

"Can I ask you something?"

"Sure. Anything for you."

"I would like to know—have you ever touched a woman's breasts before on Earth?"

Larry chuckles. "Yes, I have. Why do you ask?"

"Well, I would like to know if my breasts feel different from other women's on Earth. Would you mind doing me a favor and touching them and telling me if there is a big difference?"

"Oh. Sure, but first let me have a bit more to drink."

She smirks and nods.

He takes a few more gulps and puts down his glass. He glances at me and Ed before turning toward Claudia. Slowly, his hands go up and grab hold of her breasts. He looks like he's in Heaven.

68

He says, "I've never been asked to do this before at a party."

"So how do they feel to you, Larry? Do they feel good?"

"Let me just take another drink here first before I say anything."

I know what he's thinking. "God, help me now!"

He takes another swig then places his hands back onto her breasts. "Well, they do feel really nice to me—what I feel so far."

She appears gratified.

"Um, can I ask you a question?" he proposes. "It may not be right of me to ask this, but I have to or I think I just might die."

"Yes, you can ask me anything you want, Larry, because we are friends, are we not? You are a big boy. Just say it."

"Don't take this the wrong way, but will you have sex with me right now? I feel so hot inside and you are the only one who can help. I think I'm going to burn up if you don't say 'yes.'"

"Well, you are a man and I am a woman. I see no problem with us having sex together. That is the way it should be, don't you think?"

"Wait here just one minute, Claudia. I'll be right back."

Larry hurries over to me and Ed and asks, "Gunnar, can I use your bedroom? You have to say 'yes.' Just look at that woman over there! You cannot say 'no' to me right now do you hear? I have a chance to go to bed with her right now and this woman is like no woman on Earth and she wants me! I cannot let her go!"

I turn to Ed. He sees Larry in a way he has never seen him before and says, "I know he's married, but I'm not his father or his mother. He can make up his own mind about what he wants to do."

I tell Larry, "Take that room over there. It has a shower."

Too excited to even say, "Thank you, guys," he rushes to Claudia and tells her, "Come with me, sweetie pie—my little angel" and grabs hold of her hand and takes her to the bedroom.

Everyone sees them go but no one says a word.

Naturally, Ed and I rush to the door and place our ears against it. We hear Larry say, "I'd like to see you take off your clothes for me. But do it real slow."

I look to Ed with frustration and whisper, "What I wouldn't give to see this!"

Blanca looks over at me and I try to act natural.

"Come with me," he says.

In the office is a large computer console. He activates the monitor and switches between a few rooms until the bedroom shows up.

Larry is sitting on the bed as Claudia slowly removes her clothes. She starts with her top—one button at a time—while blowing kisses at him. It's obvious that he's dying to have sex with this woman. She throws her blouse at him and stands there with her beautiful breasts out as she moves her sexy body around for him to enjoy.

She places her leg on the bed and slowly takes off her stockings. Larry lights a cigarette. He seems to be getting rather nervous.

Each article of clothing she takes off is thrown onto him. Slowly, she lets her skirt fall to the floor and then her panties—the best part.

He stares at her beautiful nude body and face. He is not thinking of his loving wife at home with his children right now. He is only thinking of this sexy woman with him right now and what he is going to do to her in bed.

All men are the same when it comes to women. We'll all fall for any pretty lady at any time and any place.

He rises from the bed and goes to her, staring at her naked body. He kisses her breasts, then patiently and slowly, works his way to her lips and kisses them softy. He could not stop for his wife now, even if she were right there watching them make love. He wraps his arms around her and kisses all over her face and neck.

Softly, she whispers to him, "Take a shower with me. I can make you feel so good in there if you only let me."

Larry takes off his clothes and throws them to the floor. He grabs her hips and pulls her tightly against him.

She separates and pulls him toward the shower.

I say to Ed, "Please tell me there is a camera in the bathroom!"

He smirks and with a flick of a switch, we can see everything.

With water pouring over them, Larry slathers liquid soap over her naked body. She then returns the favor, which isn't as interesting to watch, to be honest. Still, what I wouldn't give to be him now.

He turns her around and lathers her back. "You're such a beautiful woman. I cannot believe this! I cannot stop loving you and your body. I feel like I'm in Heaven right now."

He kisses her neck like she was a candy he can't stop eating.

"Claudia, I'm going to make love to you in here right now."

And he does.

"It feels so good to have you inside me, Larry. Don't stop."

He presses her hard against the shower wall. There's no stopping this man now, the way he's going.

"You are hurting me, Larry. My breasts—you are squeezing them so hard." Like an animal, he doesn't care. Finally, though, he relents. He sighs and eases up.

"No, Larry, I like the pain! Don't stop! I love it so much! I have never had sex like this with a man like you. You really know how to turn a woman on with your hands and your body. You are such a good lover. I am so lucky. Earthmen really know how to do it."

She has a rather obvious orgasm.

Larry stops. "Let me dry you off with this soft towel."

That must be quite an experience for him in itself.

He then takes her to the bedroom and puts her on the bed. He lies on top of her and begins kissing her once more. He makes love to her like he knows what he's doing.

"Oh, you're hurting me again! You know that, though, don't you! We like a bit of pain. You know how to make me feel like a woman!"

He grabs her hands and pins them. She screams with pleasure.

"You have me where you want me, Larry."

He grabs her and pulls her on top of him. She cannot stop herself from having another orgasm.

"No woman on my world will feel what you are doing with me. You can have sex with me any time you want. You hear me, Larry?"

So violent is their lovemaking, they topple off the bed. Even still, Larry does not want to stop. "I just love you for this magnificent sex you are giving me!" he says as he finally finishes.

He pulls her back onto the bed and lies beside her, out of breath.

"That was some crazy sex," he tells her.

"I am glad I made you feel so happy, Larry. I never had an orgasm before. No man on my planet could do that but you gave me two!"

"I think we should put our clothes on and get back to the party."

Ed and I quickly return to the party, ourselves.

As she exits the bedroom, Claudia goes to Blanca with a big smile on her face. Larry walks over to us. "How's everything?" I ask.

"Fine. Why?"

Ed asks, "Does Claudia know you have a family back on Earth?"

Larry says, "Just look at her, so beautiful and young. Time has not yet destroyed that face or body. Her eyes, her hair—everything about her is perfect. I had to use her and I did. I loved every second and I'd do it again and again. I am a man and she is a woman. That's what a woman like her is for—not for cleaning the house or doing chores."

We give him an uneasy look.

"No one got hurt today. I'm happy and so is she. What I did was not so bad."

"Can I say something?" Ed says.

"I think I know what's coming," Larry responds.

"I understand where you're coming from. But if your wife saw a young man she really liked, would it be okay for her to have sex with him, too? After all, no one will get hurt then either, right?"

"I know she wouldn't do that because she loves me and I love her. This was just a one-time thing."

Claudia comes over and says, "Gunnar, I love your friend from Earth and I know I will be so happy with him."

Larry looks to me and Ed. He then turns to Claudia and says, "No, Claudia. We just had sex, nothing more. The truth is, I have a wife and children back home."

"What? Why didn't you say this before? You told me twice that you loved me. You lied to me?"

"When I first saw you, I just wanted to have sex with you because you are so beautiful. Any man would. It was wrong of me to use you that way. Can you forgive me?"

Claudia glares at Larry and slaps him across the face. "I hate you. I will always hate you until the day I die. I feel sorry for your wife and children to have a man like you as a husband and father.

"Gunnar, you were my friend. Why didn't you tell me?" She looks to Ed and says, "You both let me go into your bedroom with this man and said nothing."

Ed says, "I know. I should have stopped you both."

"You know, Earthman, I was so happy to come to your home. I didn't know the hurt that was waiting for me here.

"Remember the first time I saw you? I was dressed like a cowgirl in that saloon. I hugged you and you made me feel so excited. I knew that you were a good man that would not let anyone hurt me. Now I don't know if you are my friend at all anymore." She grabs her coat and storms out. I can hear crying all the way down the hall.

This hurts—knowing that my friend was hurt by my other friend. And I can't help but feel partially responsible. After all, I am the one who encouraged Larry when we first got here.

No one says a word, although the tension in the room is obvious. Everyone looks at Larry and at me with unease.

"I need another drink," I say. I get a glass, fill it with whiskey and guzzle it down.

Blanca walks over to me and says, "I cannot stay here any longer and you know why, Gunnar. Thank you, Ed, for asking me to come. Good-bye, Gunnar. She does not say a word to Larry as she pulls out her conductor and disappears.

Sarah also approaches and says to Ed, "Thank you for inviting me but I, too, have to go and you know why. You understand. Good-bye, Gunnar. Have a good flight back to Planet X, Larry."

She takes out her conductor and is gone as well.

Ed comments, "So not much of a party anymore. Thanks, Larry! I thought you said no one got hurt here today. Was it worth it?"

"I'm sorry, but I'm only human. You *did* see what she looks like! How could I stop myself? She really wanted me. If I passed that up, I would have regretted it the rest of my life. You told me, Gunnar, that what I do on this planet is up to me. I'm safe because these women live on another planet. 'Have some fun! You're a big boy now!'"

I ask, "Are you going to tell your wife?"

"You crazy? She'd leave me in a minute! She must never know about this. You hear me?"

Ed asks, "Why did you come all the way out here, anyway?"

"I just wanted to know that you were okay. You are still my best friend, aren't you?"

"Yeah, I'm doing well and I can take care of myself. I don't need you looking after me. Next time, maybe you should just stay home." He then pauses and says, "And yeah, you are still my best friend."

As I get another drink—that I now desperately need—I ask Ed, "So what are you doing with yourself? You have a job?"

"Yes, Governor John helped me out. I fly their UFO—that's what we call it here as a joke—to Earth, transporting criminals there."

"Cool. Hey, I won't be able to sleep. Let's head out to the saloon. We'll just walk so I can clear my head."

"How about it Larry?" Ed asks.

"A good walk and a drink is exactly what I need right now, too."

We take the long walk to the saloon. Larry marvels over being on another world, as I once did.

We go inside this bar I know so well and I say 'hi' to the owner. "Toby, this is my friend, Larry. He's from Earth as well."

"Greetings, Larry. Welcome to my establishment. I hope you have a good time. What can I get you Earthmen to drink?"

"Three glasses and a bottle of whiskey," I tell him.

"You got it. Coming right up."

Soon enough, we're drinking whiskey and talking, just like the old days back in Florida.

An ugly man steps up and says, "I thought I smelled something bad in here. Then I looked up and saw you Earthmen. That explains it. I hate Earthmen. I wish all of them were dead."

"Mister, we're not looking for any trouble," I tell him.

He says, "I know you're not looking for trouble with me because I'll kick your ass and you know it, you piece of shit. That is how you smell. Like a piece of shit. All three of you and you know it, too."

Now I've had it. I stand up and look him in the eye. "I don't want to hurt you but I will if you keep it up. You may not know this, but I'm one mean asshole in a fight, so you better watch it with me."

"I know I'm all alone here but I don't care. I can still kick all three of your asses without breaking a sweat."

"Why do you want to fight with us so bad?" I ask.

"Because my little sister was so happy to go to your home tonight, Gunnar—yeah, I know who you are—that's all she talked about. But you just used her for sex like the wild animals that you are. My little sister is a good girl. She came home crying after what you did to her."

Larry shrinks in his seat.

"So, what'll it be?" the man threatens. "One at a time or all three at once? Here or outside? Either way, you're all dead meat to me."

"What's your name?" I ask.

"Call me Greg."

"Greg, your sister is a good person and I call her my friend."

He abruptly hits me in the face but my revealer protects me.

Ed immediately bursts up from his chair. "No, Ed. I can take care of this myself."

Greg hits me again and I say to Ed, "I can take it. Stay cool."

"Greg, let me say something. When I'm done, I'll fight if you still want to, but you will lose. You have my word on that."

"Hurry up, 'cause your ass is mine, Gunnar."

"Greg, I've never had sex with your sister. She will tell you that. And my friend here, Ed, has never had sex with her either. The fact is, you would be fighting two people that are actually her friends.

"However, Larry here he did have sex with your sister."

Greg says, "If that's so, I will definitely be kicking his ass, and thank you for telling me that. Stand up, Larry. Let's go outside."

"But I'm still talking, Greg."

"Get on with it! I got some ass-kicking to do!"

"As I was saying, my friend did ask your sister to have sex with him and she did say 'yes' to him. If she had only asked him if he was married during the five minutes prior to meeting him, he would have told her so. Afterwards, he did volunteer this information to her. Now, you tell me, was what my friend did that was really so bad?"

"They only knew each other five minutes?"

"I'm afraid so."

Larry adds, "I'm not proud of what I did and I'm sorry for hurting your sister. I do care about her. I did wrong and I will tell my wife. She should know what kind of man she married."

"Maybe I should think before I pick fights, then," Greg confesses. "I could have gotten my butt kicked for nothing."

"Let's call it a night," Ed suggests.

We get back home and look around at all the mess from the party. Seating ourselves on the couch, Ed says, "Tomorrow I'm headed on a big ship into outer space. You two can come if you want."

"Yeah, I'd like to go. How about it, Larry?"

"I *should* go home and confess everything to my wife. But I'm not looking forward to getting killed. So, yeah, I'll go with you."

"Let's get some sleep, then," Ed says. "We leave at 5:00 am."

Chapter 8: **The Mother Ship**

Come morning, everyone is up and ready to go.

Ed says, "I need to make some arrangements for you guys to come aboard. How about we meet at your time machine shortly?"

"Okay, we'll see you in a few," I tell him.

Ed takes out his conductor and clicks it. In a blink, he is gone.

After some breakfast I say, "Well, you ready to go, Larry?"

"As ready as any man could be to leave this planet."

"I walk to Larry, look uncomfortably at him for a minute and say, "Okay, give me your hand."

He reluctantly places his palm in mine as I pull out my conductor. He nods and I press the magic button. In an instant, we arrive at my time machine.

Looking around us, I notice other time machines parked nearby. Some appear quite gleaming and modern, unlike mine. But who cares. Ole Nelly may be old but she's still good to me.

I turn to discover Ed approaching. "I spoke to my captain on the mother ship and he said it was okay for you two to come with us."

"The way you spoke, I thought you were the captain," I remark.

"I'm just a pilot."

"Oh, I see."

"The spaceship is so huge that people actually live there for years at a time and go to school there, too. It even has a park. And you can buy anything there—clothes, furniture—you name it, they got it. Just follow me. I'll be flying my own transport ship over there." He grins. "Try to keep up if you can or I'll have to leave you behind."

I chuckle. Larry and I get into our time machine and power up.

Ed takes off and I follow. He sure is going fast! He's an astronaut, not a jet pilot! His craft leaves the atmosphere in a big ball of fire but I know he's okay. They know how to build a quality spaceship here. Soon, we're on fire, too, as we make our way into outer space.

Up ahead I see a massive spaceship. It looks like a giant building in the sky. Ed flies within it.

I hear a calm, female voice say, "Please stop your engines and let us bring you aboard if you please."

Gently, we glide closer. A giant door opens for us and we float in. They set us down next to Ed's ship. Nelly's doors open. We get out and look about this giant machine. I see many warships in here, too. If they ever got in a fight, they would certainly be ready.

Ed says, "First off, let me show you around."

Walking through this astounding spacecraft, Ed remarks, "That's a good bar right there. They have good beer."

I open their door and peek in.

"My kind of place, then," I comment.

"That's why I mention it."

"And I hope my kind of beer," Larry remarks.

"Over there is the park I told you about. It has a playground with real grass and trees. But let's go on deck and meet the captain."

We follow Ed to an elevator and get off on the tenth level. Ed says to a man standing at the elevator, "Permission to see the captain?"

The man looks to a man who appears to be the captain, who nods. "Permission granted. Welcome aboard, sir."

Large monitors on the surrounding walls display views from every side of the ship. Watching them are about forty busy officers.

Larry, Ed and I walk to this man wearing a formal suit and beard. Ed addresses him. "Captain Mills, these men have come from Earth. This is Larry, an astronaut friend of mine."

"Welcome aboard, Larry. Ah, and I know this man. Gunnar Best!"

"How did you know that, sir?" I inquire.

"You are the first Earthman to come to our planet, are you not?"

An officer yells, "Captain! A craft approaches starboard."

"Williams, find out who's onboard and how many!"

"Sir, I read ten Gettion and fifteen Earthlings."

The captain pauses. "Establish audio contact."

78

Williams gives the captain a look of surprise.

"Let it be done! And don't look at me like that!"

"Yes, sir. A link has been opened."

"This is Captain Mills. Who am I addressing?"

A harsh and raspy voice replies. "I am Captain Rota. We are here in peace. We do not want any trouble with you, Captain."

"What are you doing with earthlings on your ship?"

"Just transporting them to our planet."

"For what purpose?"

"Anatomy practice for our young doctors, of course."

"Stop your engines immediately."

There is silence for several seconds. "Of course."

I whisper to Ed, "Why are they doing what our captain says?"

"Because we can blow 'em away with one shot and they know it."

"Then why is everyone on the bridge so tense?"

"Because none of them have ever seen a Gettion before."

On one of the large screens, I watch the Gettion spacecraft enter the landing bay and set down close to my time machine.

Captain Mills asks me, "Would you like to go and see the aliens?"

"I would, yes."

We follow the caption into the elevator and head down.

I ask him, "Would you mind at all if I spoke with one of them on my own? I'd like to know what business they have with my people."

"I would appreciate it if you would, Gunnar. We can monitor your safety through our extensive security systems."

We reach the lowest deck. The alien ship looks very small down here compared to the immense size of the docking bay.

Its door starts to open. After a moment, several aliens come out. They have a classic alien appearance with large heads and huge eyes. One is wearing a silver suit. Another is dressed in a gold suit. He says, "You must be Captain Mills, sir."

"What are you doing with so many humans, Captain Rodta?"

"Just taking them to my planet, sir. Nothing more, sir."

"I want to see them."

"But, Captain, they are asleep. I do not wish to wake them."

"I don't care if they're sleeping! I want to see them now, Rodta!"

In a language I don't understand, Captain Rodta says something to the alien in silver.

Loudly, I say to Ed, "I think I'll go have a beer. I'll see you later. Any of you Gettion care to join me?"

A sly look comes over Rodta's face. He says to one of his crew, "Why don't you join our Antonion friend for a drink."

"It would be my pleasure, sir."

Captain Mills pretends to be disapproving as we walk off.

We head to the bar Ed pointed out earlier. It's actually quite huge. It looks like it could hold a thousand people. It has many pictures on the walls and pretty lights all over. We sit at the bar where I ask the bartender, "May I have a beer for me and my friend here?"

"Two beers coming right up, sir." I can see in his eyes that he is not too happy with this alien being here.

He brings our drinks and says, "Your imprint, please." He directs my attention to a computer panel which has an outline of a hand on it. I place my palm onto it and payment for our beverages is instantly deducted from my Antonion bank account.

"So what's your name?" I ask the alien.

"Wata."

"That's what I said."

"Wata is the name."

"You tell me."

He appears frustrated.

I tell him, "I'll just call you 'Bob.' That okay with you?"

"Fine," he responds—although he doesn't really seem very happy about it. "And your name is?"

"Gunnar Best."

"Do you live on Antonion?"

"I have a nice apartment there."

"Seems like every other day some captain stops us to inspect the humans we have stored in our spacecraft before they let us go. What's the big deal? They're only earthlings. Every day's the same old thing. At least this time I'm up here drinking with you."

"What do you do with the humans?"

"Our doctors-in-training perform operations on them so they can get good before they operate on us. And they pay very well for them."

"But couldn't the humans die on the operating table?"

"So what? I'm not going to cry for any human. They are not like real people; like us. And they're easy enough to replace. I don't even think about it anymore. They're just money to me. A man has to work to live, you know. I got a wife and kid. They have to eat."

"I heard that you often pick the same people over and over again. Is that true?"

"Yes. We plant a computer chip in their heads beneath their hair, under their skin. It's too small for them to see or feel because we have good doctors on our planet. With that, we always know where they are and can pick them up anytime we want to."

"That's pretty clever of you guys."

"You know, Gunnar, one day we'll own the Earth. It will be ours. You wait and see."

The bartender returns and gives the Gettion a dirty look. He then paints on a smile and asks, "Another round for you two?"

"Yes, please," I calmly respond. I reach for the imprint panel but the bartender tells me, "I already have your imprint, sir. Thank you."

"Bob, I would like to know, what gives you the idea that one day you'll own the Earth?"

"We already have people there that look exactly like Earth people. You could never tell by looking at them. Although, they do have this mark on their neck—like mine, see?"

It resembles an "S" or a snake.

"Why is that, I ask?"

81

"Basically, it's because they are part human and part Gettion. All of us have it and it won't go away no matter how hard we try. It's a small gland that our body needs. Without it, we die."

I try to act disinterested. "Huh."

"Gunnar, you will like this: if our Gettion are not totally gorgeous, they cannot go to Earth. When a man of ours goes to a bar, the women want to go to bed with him any way they can. He does not use any protection because we want her to get pregnant. The women do not care what kind of man he is. If you told them he was an alien from another planet and their child will one day take over the world, they still wouldn't give a damn because Earth women don't think."

"What about the women you send?"

"Same thing. They are always very beautiful. Any man would go to bed with one of them in a minute. She gets pregnant but gives birth on one of our ships. We have it all worked out."

"Well, we better get back before it gets too late."

As we head back down on the elevator, I notice the alien looking at my clothing with a confused expression.

Arriving at the hanger, a number of groggy people are coming out of the Gettion ship. The women have little clothing on, as though they were asleep when the aliens got them. The men are mostly in shorts and t-shirts. There is one man and woman with no clothes on at all.

"What are we doing here?" a woman asks.

Captain Mills says to me in the Antonion language, "Talk to them, Gunner. I can't speak your language now but will in a few minutes. Tell them the truth about what is happening to them. I'll be back."

"Yes, sir."

As he departs, I say to them, "My name is Gunnar Best. You're in outer space on a large ship in another solar system. You were brought here by those aliens. They are taking you to their planet so surgeons can operate on you for practice. Many of you will die in the process."

A man shouts, "I won't stand for this! I have a lot of money. I can pay anything they want. Just tell them that for me."

82

"Mister, your money is no good out here. Your body is the only thing they want from you."

"Who can I report this to?"

"There are no police here in outer space. You need to understand that if you say the wrong thing here, you are a dead man. Don't talk. Just listen. You understand?"

An attractive woman with red hair asks, "Can you help us?"

"I don't know what I can do."

Captain Mills returns. "Thank you, Gunnar," he states in English. He turns to the Gettion and says, "I want them to understand what we are saying about them. I know you speak English. It is, after all, their lives on the line.

Rodta says in English, "These people belong to me. I found them on Earth and they are mine to do with as I please. You have no right to intervene and you know it."

"On this ship, nobody tells me what I can or cannot do."

The earthlings cannot believe their ears.

Rodta says, "Our doctors need these humans for scientific testing of new medicine and procedures. Our work here will save many lives. Do you want to stand in the way of that?"

"I understand your needs but I don't approve of your methods."

The humans look to Captain Mills and me with concern. Some of the women start to cry. A few men begin to sob as well. They know that this meeting will decide their fate.

Captain Mills says, "Gunnar here is not from either of our worlds. We will stand by his decision. They will live or die by his word."

The captives look to me, knowing that their lives are in my hands. I cannot let them perish on operation tables like animals.

Rodta says, "Gunnar, my friend, I have seen you looking at that pretty woman over there with the red hair. I can tell you like her. She does have a nice body. You will like her a lot better in bed. You do not need her permission out here in space and she knows it—or will in time. I will give her to you and you can do anything you want to her."

"I'm not going to lie, Rodta. She does have an outstanding body."
She scans me from head to toe. She thinks she will need to have sex
with me or die and she can't do a thing about it. "But I must say 'no.'
My father once said, 'If it doesn't belong to you, you can't touch it.'
She is not my woman so I cannot touch her."

"But you can have any woman here. Just say so. Your father will
not have to know what we do out here. He is not here, is he?"

All the women look to me. I can see in the redhead's eyes that she
wants me to say "yes" over being killed on an operating table. She is
frightened as she stands there half-naked and shaking from the cold.

I take off my coat, put it on her and softly say, "No one will hurt
you. You have my word."

She lifts up her head, looks me in the eye and states with a smile,
"I do believe you, Gunnar."

I turn to Rodta and say, "We do not have a deal. That woman has
rights and I can't take those rights away from her or any person here.
She is human, like me, and I have to respect that."

"Human?" he shouts.

Bob looks to me with surprise and betrayal.

"No one has the right to take human life and if I have anything to
say about it, no one will. She might have children someday and they
have the right to be born and live. I cannot let you take that from her
or them for a few tests."

"Think about this…" Rodta says in a threatening tone.

I tell him, "I always wanted to be a doctor, myself. Now I can be!
Captain, may I operate on Rodta and do some test of my own?"

"If you want to, Gunnar. I see nothing wrong with it if it will save
many human lives. We have the perfect place where you can operate."

"You have no right to operate on me!" Rodta protests. "There are
laws against what you are doing. I have rights. I'm a Gettion captain!"

"But I am the Captain of this ship! What I say here is law and you
know that, Rodta. I agreed to let him decide. If he wants to operate on
you, then so be it."

"But I have a life! I'm important!"

I say, "You will be my first operation but I promise to do my best. The first thing I want to see is your heart in my hand and see if it's in good condition. If it is, I will put it back in your chest."

"This is outrageous!"

"All doctors have to start somewhere and today I'll start with you. I could be a good doctor for all you know."

"I want to live!"

I tell him, "Now you know what these humans must go through. You say you want to operate on these humans but you say it is wrong for me to operate on you. To me, you are a Gettion and not a human. I see nothing wrong here if you should die on the operating table. I will simply get another Gettion to operate on until I get it right."

"This is illegal!"

"Rodta, I will make you a deal and I think you will like it. If you release these humans, I will not operate on you and let you go home."

Rodta grins slyly.

"Oh, and I know about the chips in their heads. You will remove those before they go home. I will be sure to find out where they live, too, in case they go missing later. If I find out that one of them has been taken, I'm going to get real mad. You don't want to see me mad. By the time I cool down, a lot of Gettion will be dead."

"We are all over the galaxy. How is it that you could find us?"

"Not hard for me and my trusty 45. Besides, you and I both know that many Gettion are already on my planet and can be identified by the 'S' on their necks. Should I find one, they will die by my hand."

Rodta glares at me and then smiles. "You have a deal."

"Sir," I tell Captain Mills, "let them go."

He nods. "Leave your engines off. We will control your craft."

The Gettion enter their ship and are sent away.

"Captain, why did you put me in charge instead of Ed? He works with you and I don't."

"Because I know what kind of person you are, Gunnar."

"We just met."

He leans in close and whispers, "John, the Governor, is my friend. I reviewed his time logs on you and I know your history with a man named Jack. He said you would be a good time traveler because you know how to talk to people. It's true. I saw that today."

I go to the girl with the long, red hair. "What's your name?"

"Jennifer. Thank you for looking out for us. I couldn't believe that creep offered my body to you like that. I thought you were going to do it for a minute there."

"You see, Jennifer, that was just a business deal. You only mean money to them. If I had lied to them, they would have known.

"Captain, can we get some clothes for these people?"

"Fisher, see to it."

"Yes, Captain. Come with me, please," he tells the humans.

An hour later, I'm in my quarters and hear a knock at my door. I open it to find Jennifer. "Here's your jacket, Gunnar. It smells nice."

"Would you like to get something to eat or drink?"

"A drink would be good right now."

I put my jacket on and we walk to my new favorite bar. Sitting at a table, I ask the waitress for a beer. Jennifer asks for a cup of coffee, very hot. She is surprised that they actually have it out here in space.

"Where do you live, Gunnar?"

"El Sobrante, California. You?"

"I live right across the bay in San Francisco! I work at T.A. Bank of San Francisco on Geary Street. What do you do?"

The waitress returns with our beverages and I place my hand upon the imprint panel to pay.

"Thank you, sir," she says with a big smile as she departs.

"What was that board for?" Jennifer asks.

"It's how they pay for stuff out here. It's like swiping a credit card back on Earth.

"Anyway, I don't really have a job right now."

"Well, you saved my life so I'm going help you find one."

"I used to have normal jobs but didn't like it too much. I had this boss once named Sam that nobody really liked. He would talk to you like you were a machine and not a person. He never used your name. 'You do this or that.' Never 'Gunnar, can you do is for me?'"

"We all have to work with people like that at some point in life."

"One time I went outside for something and when I came back, he told me those front doors are for customers and I needed to go down and use these other doors instead. It was two o'clock in the morning! The place was closed! That guy had a screw loose I think."

"Yeah, but some turn out to be friends."

"There was one nice girl that worked there. She used to bring us all homemade chocolate chip cookies. Her brother worked there, too.

"We'll have to find you a job with more nice people, then."

"Jennifer, soon you'll be home with your loved ones. We'll put you back in your bed and all memories of this will be wiped clean."

"I won't remember you?"

"This makes it safe for me to tell you the truth. You see, Jennifer, I'm a time traveler. I can go anywhere in time—the past or the future. It's all up to me. So I don't really need to work anymore. I have quite a lot of money now, actually. You could say I've developed a knack for picking stocks that do well down the road."

With sad eyes she asks, "Gunnar, can I kiss you in here?"

"Yes, you may. I would like that very much."

She presses her lips against mine and looks deep into my eyes. "You're a good kisser, Gunnar. Still want to have sex with me?"

"I'd like to, but I must decline your offer. I think you only want to because I saved your life. There's no charge for that."

"I'm going to forget all this anyway, so why not just do it?"

"One day I will walk into your bank and I will talk to you there. We'll see what happens then."

"Gunnar, your voice sounds so sweet when you talk to me, but so harsh when you spoke to those aliens."

"It comes with the territory out here."

"Can I at least hold your hand for right now? The truth is, I'm still shaking from everything that just happened. That's why I really want you close to me. I thought I would never die, but today I know I can."

I move my chair close to her and wrap my arm around her. She starts to sob on my shoulder and squeeze my hand tightly around her.

"If those aliens come back to my home, what can I do without you there to save me again?"

"Don't worry, I already warned them about that."

Ed and Larry show up. Ed says, "It's time to send her back home. But first the doctor wants to take that chip from her head."

"Gunnar, can you go with me?"

"I'll stick with you all the way home. How about that."

She does not want to let go of my hand as we walk to the doctor.

At the medical facility, the nurse sits Jennifer in a big chair where the doctor painlessly removes the chip from her head.

"Young lady, you are okay now to return to Earth," he says with a comforting smile.

She turns to me with a sad face.

A few hours later, we are ready to depart in Ed's transport ship. All of us earthlings are aboard and very happy to be going back home. Jennifer and I sit together near a window as we take off.

The trip goes pretty quickly. A bit too quickly for me, actually, as I wish I can have more time with her. But it has to end sooner or later.

As we approach our planet, Ed says over the loudspeaker, "Now is a good time for all of you to change back into your Earth clothes."

Soon after, Ed takes the ship into the atmosphere and each person is returned to their rightful homes, with only Jennifer left. She tells Ed where she lives and we swiftly arrive there in our invisible spacecraft.

Before she is sent off, she is laid onto a table where Ed places a device over her head.

"Good-bye, Jennifer," I tell her, "and good luck out there."

"Gunnar, please don't let go of my hand. I know I'll never forget you in my heart."

Ed activates the machine and she slips into a deep sleep.

"See this red light?" Ed says. "It means her latest memories have all been erased. All she'll remember is going to bed the night before. Let go of her hand now so we can transfer her down to her bedroom. Do you want to go with us?"

"I told her I'd stick with her all the way home."

Ed presses a button on his belt and we are instantly transferred to her room. Hovering over her bed, she is gently lowered and looks like an angel lying there. I cover her up and kiss her forehead. "Good-bye, Jennifer. I have to go but I'll see you again. You have my word on it.

"Let's go, Ed. I can't take any more of this."

Hours later, we begin docking with the mother ship. The calming voice says, "Stop your engines and let us pull you in if you please."

Once safely docked, we get out and I feel relieved to see my time machine again, still parked where I left her.

We report to the bridge. "Captain," I say, "I'm leaving now."

"Gunnar, it has been a pleasure having you on board."

"Thank you, sir. I do have one question for you."

"What is it?"

"You quoted something Jack said to me back in Tombstone. Yet, no one else was there. How did you know what he told me?"

"I guess John did not tell you about that ring on your finger there. When you wear it, every word you say is recorded on his computer."

"Really? Yes, he neglected to mention that."

"He keeps his eyes on all time travelers. That is part of his job; to see that nothing happens to you. When you first met him, you did ask a lot of questions. He probably just forgot to tell you or assumed Jack knew about it and already told you about it before. If you just take the ring off your finger, the recording will stop."

"Hmm."

"Think of it this way, if you find yourself in trouble and have no way out, John can still send help. That's one of the reasons for it."

"Thanks for everything, Captain. Larry and I must be going back home where we belong. So long and take care of Ed for me."

"Safe travels."

Back inside my time machine, we relax as the mother ship guides us out from the docking bay.

Staring at the stars, Larry says, "I feel so bad about what I did at your apartment. But at least I learned to think with my head instead of with my penis. At the same time, though, I don't really feel bad about having sex with her at all."

"That's not hard to understand."

"It was the best sex I ever had. I cannot get her out of my mind! Her body… it's a sex machine. She has everything a man could want. That face was so beautiful to look at when I was on top of her and when she was on top of me. I'll never forget her smile as she moved her body and climaxed. Only once in a lifetime does a man get any kind of chance like that. I had to do it or I would've died."

"I wanted a woman like that once. She actually said to me one day that she knew it and wanted me, too. She said that my best friend, Tom, would be two hours late from work and wanted to go wild with me. She put my hand on her breast—which felt so good—and put my other hand on her hip. I looked into her eyes and they were filled with passion. But I told her I couldn't live with myself if I did that with my best friend's girl and just walked away. Sometimes, though, I wonder about the sex we could've had. I know it would've been the best ever. All men are slaves to our penises. We can never truly be set free of it. We're always looking for the next woman."

"Uh-oh," Larry utters.

I look out and see six spaceships moving in front of us. I stop us and wait to see what will happen next.

"Are those more Gettion?" Larry asks.

"Either way, they don't look too friendly."

A voice comes over the communications system. "We have you. There is nowhere you can go. Surrender to us or die."

I tell them, "I may live in California, but I was born in Texas and we are some serious bad-asses. Six of your ships ain't enough to bring down one Texan so you better get more help."

"You will surrender to us or die where you are."

I flip open a box between our seats, exposing the weapon controls. I grip the steering wheel and then start to fire my guns while whipping us around and around. Each of their ships are struck and destroyed.

"Damn!" Larry says. "That was amazing! How did you do that?"

"It's not that hard fighting spaceships out here if you play a lot of video games.

"Let's go home."

Chapter 9: **Forget Me Not**

Fast approaching Earth, I slow down and bring us into orbit until positioned over San Francisco. Flames blaze over the red-hot skin of our outer hull as Nelly descends. "Easy does it there, old girl." I know that if she can survive a dinosaur-age lava flow, she can take this, too.

Now well within Earth's atmosphere, we finally arrive back home. Larry's car is still parked out in front of our house.

Larry says, "I know you wanted to stay longer and I screwed it up for you and everyone else. I wanted to stay, too, and get to know that world. I am an astronaut, after all. I guess I can't really blame Ed for wanting to stay. He's happy there and I'm happy for him."

"We'll go back someday. You wait and see."

Now on the ground, the doors start to open up for us.

"Want to come in for a while?"

"No, I'd better get back to my wife. She has a right to know the truth about me and my love affair."

"You know, Larry, I am not going to say a word. You know that, right? It's really up to you if you tell her. She's going to be very hurt, though. It might even destroy your marriage."

"Yeah, I know. I've thought about it and just feel I've got to tell her the truth or I won't be able to live with myself. That's really what marriage is all about—the truth, not lies."

"She loves you now, but after you tell her she's going to hate you. That love may be gone forever. Really think about that before you say anything. I wouldn't know what to do with the mess you're in but at least you'll still be my friend. You know that."

"Thanks, Gunnar. I'll let you know what happens. Bye."

Larry walks through the side yard to his car and drives away.

I turn to my time machine and it is also gone now, so I go into the house. Debbie and my brother, James, ask how everything went.

"Oh, it went great! We had no problems at all. Just one big happy family over there. Had a real good time."

"Why did you come back so soon?" Debbie asks.

"Larry missed his wife too much."

"That's beautiful. It's hard to find a man who really loves his wife like that. You guys could learn something from him."

"Yes, Debbie. I have to get some sleep now."

In the morning, I get up and go downstairs. I find my brother and Debbie drinking coffee in the kitchen, about to leave for work.

Debbie asks, "What's your plan for today?"

"I'm going out to San Francisco and see someone special."

"To have some fun?" she asks.

"I hope so. We will see."

A couple of hours later, I cross the Bay Bridge and head for Geary Street. That must be the bank. I park my pick-up in front.

I walk inside and find Jennifer sitting at her desk, sipping a coffee. "Here I am! Gunnar!"

She frowns. "Can I help you, sir?"

"It's Gunnar!"

"You said that already. Can I help you?"

"You said you would never forget me and you did. But here I am like I promised."

"Sir, you have me mixed up with somebody else. Take my word, I have never met you before in my life."

A man walks up and asks, "Is this man bothering you, Jennifer?"

"No, he was just leaving."

He stares me down and walks away, keeping a close eye on me. A lot of other people are glaring at me as well.

"Jennifer, I'll go out those doors and you'll never see me again if that's what you want. However, I know you went to bed last night as you always do but right now are still very tired. I can tell you why."

She appears confused and intrigued.

"Because you were with me all night. And you said you wanted to see me again and I told you I would come. I kept my word, Jennifer.

"It'll be noon in a few more minutes. I'm going to that restaurant next door. After that, I'll be gone for good."

As I walk out, I can feel her watching me.

Entering the restaurant, I locate a table and sit next to the window. The waitress asks, "Can I take your order, sir?"

"Yes, I would like a cup of coffee, a hamburger and a piece of pie. Any pie will do, as long it is pie, young lady."

"I'll be right back with that, sir."

A short while later, she returns with my food. As I pick up my cup of coffee, I see Jennifer standing there with a faint smile. Hesitantly, she approaches. "May I sit, Gunnar? See, I remembered your name."

"What kept you so long? It's not that far from the bank."

"I wasn't sure if I should come."

"It's nice to see you again, Jennifer."

"Tell me what happened last night. I did wake up exhausted."

"I'll tell you but you won't believe me."

"Try me."

"Well, I was on a giant spaceship speaking with the Captain when we captured another craft and brought it into our hanger. Everyone in it was ordered out and that's when I first saw you. You were abducted so alien doctors could operate on you and runs tests. The Captain put your fate in my hands. The aliens offered you to me. I'm not going to lie but I did express some interest, though I refused on the basis that you had basic rights. Then I gave you my jacket and we went out for drinks after. You offered yourself to me for saving you but I said that wasn't necessary. We then took you home and put a device on your head so you would forget everything that happened."

"If you expect me to believe all that, you're crazy in the head."

"It hurts me to hear you say that but I guess if I saw the others, they'd treat me like dirt, too. At any rate, if you ever need my help, Jennifer, I'll be there for you. You can count on it."

"Thank you, but I won't need it. I'm a big girl and can take care of myself. But thanks anyway."

"I was not talking to you. I was talking to the other Jennifer inside of you. She will always be my friend."

"Better eat your food before it gets cold."

"I'm not hungry anymore."

"Well, if that's it, I'll be going now. Bye, crazy man. I don't ever want to see you again, understand?"

She gets up and leaves.

I understand her perspective, but I can't help but feel hurt.

I pay my bill and head back home.

A woman doesn't need a knife to cut a man. The words from her lips alone are enough to do the job. They go straight through his heart and kill him from the inside.

Two weeks pass but I still cannot get Jennifer out of my mind for some reason.

Back at Jennifer's house, she goes to bed as usual and falls asleep. A hand touches her and she wakes to find an alien placing something over her head. Instantly, she is rendered unconscious. They put her in a sealed pod and take her far away from her home into outer space.

They take Jennifer out and wake her up. Seeing the strange aliens, she screams. They throw her onto the floor and kick her. One of them strikes her face and utters in English, "I hate seeing these animals in clothes." They tear them off. She tries to cover herself with her arms.

"Do you know where you and your friends are going? Soon, you will be at a medical college on my planet where students will study your body and run many experiments. If they want to study your eyes, they will just take them out. If they want to look at your heart, they will just remove that, too. You will give them much practice before you die on that cold table of theirs."

"You can't do this! We are human beings!"

"It pays my bills. What's wrong with that? And yes, you are only human. It's not like you're real people, like us. I know on your world, you dissect animals to learn from them. We do the same here but use humans like you instead."

"I should have listened to you, Gunnar," she mutters to herself.

"Most people here will only live for a week or two. If you want to live longer, I can tell you how."

"I'm listening."

"Just have sex with the human males we have here."

"How can that help me live longer?"

"If you become pregnant, they won't operate on you. They would rather wait and operate on your child. When you arrive, you will all be in the same cage together getting cleaned up with lots of soap and water—because you humans are such filthy things. That will be your chance. The doctors will see this and have you do it again and again until you are pregnant. If a man does not want to, go to another. Your life will depend on it. The doctors will check if you are pregnant."

"You're monsters!"

"After you get cleaned up, they will shave all the hair from your body so they can operate on you. You will have to work fast. Don't tell the men that they will soon be dead or they won't perform well."

Back on Earth, I go to bed but can't sleep. I have this odd feeling that something is wrong. I keep thinking about Jennifer.

I get up and get dressed. Outside, I climb in my time machine and head for San Francisco. I see her house below and begin my descent. There's something strange in here. I'm sure something has happened. There is a mess on the floor, but only in her bedroom. From the trunk of my time machine, I pull my guns and make sure they're loaded.

Blasting out of the atmosphere, Nelly and I hurdle through space. Eventually, I detect a spaceship up ahead. It's the same kind that had Jennifer before. They try to lose me but I manage to stay on them.

On my dashboard is a green button with a small cover that reads, "AUTO-PURSUE." I flip the cover off. On the computer monitor, there is a target symbol which I aim over the symbol of their ship. I push the auto-pursue button and an object launches after them. A few seconds later, a light on the dashboard goes on and off. There is now a red light over the Gettion craft on my monitor, which is also locked in on the middle of the screen with the target symbol over it.

I follow them into another solar system. Here, I see another world that's a lot different from my own.

Using my conductor, I place a call to the Governor of Antonion. "John, it's Gunnar. How are you?"

"Gunnar! I was just thinking of you and here you are calling me!"

"I want to ask you a question about my time machine. Can it take a bullet or something much worse if I were hit?"

"Oh, yes. It has a two-foot thick, near-impenetrable force field to protect you. Remember when you were submerged in hot lava? It was this that kept you safe. Why do you ask?"

"I think I may be getting into a fight out here with the Gettion."

"Where are you?"

"I think I'm at their home planet. They have a friend of mine and I've got to get her out of there or they'll kill her for sure."

"Do you need help?"

"No, I think I can handle it myself this time, John. You don't need to get involved but thank you anyway."

"If you find that you do need assistance, just give me a call."

"Thanks, John. Good-bye."

"I enter the atmosphere with my invisibility shield activated. The auto-pursue system leads me to a large building surrounded by many smaller ones. Their spaceship remains dead ahead.

I take my book of languages and locate "Gettion – 3103." I punch the numbers into the dashboard and a light goes on and off. Just like that, I can now speak their language.

They land behind what appears to be a large campus of some kind. It must be the medical school that Bob told me about. I settle to the ground and see a number of humans being herded inside. They are all completely naked now. I slowly glide over to them. Jennifer is among them and yes, she does looks good—safe, I mean.

In the school, I locate the room where the humans are being kept. I look around and I see no Gettion around at the moment. I move in a bit closer and open my door. Everyone freezes. I step out and close it. They start to move normally again.

Jennifer sees me. "Oh, my God! What are you doing out here?"

"Feel like leaving? Next stop, planet Earth!"

"But what about the others?"

"I can only take three in my ship. You and one more person."

"We can't just let them to die out here on this planet, Gunnar! We have to do something for them. It's the human thing to do."

"Does anyone here know how to fly a plane?" I ask.

"I do," a man says. "But not a UFO."

"You'll learn if you want to live. What's your name?"

"Taylor."

"How do you do, Taylor. I'm Gunnar. Know how to use a gun?"

"Yes."

I hand him one of my handguns. "It's loaded. Shoot to kill, got it? Here's a knife, too. Jennifer, stay here. We'll be back for the rest of you shortly if I'm not killed first."

Taylor remains naked as he and I climb inside my time machine. The doors close and we become invisible.

A Gettion enters. He begins hosing down the humans and dowses them with a kind of soap. The water hits them hard, causing some to fall, including Jennifer. But there's nothing I can do about it now. We float outside to the Gettion ship and I punch 3103 into the dashboard."

"What was that light?" he asks.

"It means you are now capable of speaking Gettion."

"How can a light help me speak their language?"

"I wish I knew how to answer that, but you'll see."

We get out. The door is open to the Gettion craft so we go in and look around. There is just one alien aboard, sitting with his back to us. I sneak up behind him and say, "Move and you're dead. Teach my friend how to fly this thing or you'll die right now. Hear me?"

The alien sees Taylor's naked body and chuckles. I see a coat and give it to him to cover himself with.

With his newfound language, Taylor asks many questions about the ship. Before long, he says, "I think I can fly this spaceship now."

"Good. I'll get the others. I say to the Gettion, "Get up and come with me." We go out and I strike him with my gun, sending him to the ground. I'd kill him but he did help us, I suppose.

I hurry to the others. One of them asks, "Can we go home now?"

"We're going to try to get you all back home if we can."

An alien unexpectedly enters and goes for his weapon. In a blink, I pull mine and gun him down. I lunge for his keys and open the cage. Another Gettion bursts in. I shoot him as well. Soon, more arrive but my gun is doing a fine job so far. In fact, I'm starting to enjoy this.

We manage to get out safely and fight our way to the Gettion ship where Taylor stands outside. "Okay," I tell him, "Get them out of here and don't stop for anyone! I'll be behind you shortly."

I reload my gun as he closes the door behind me.

The revealer in my pocket creates a powerful shield around me. The aliens open fire, but their lasers cannot penetrate. I, however, can still shoot them just fine with my 45.

On the run, I push on my ring and my time machine materializes. I have never had so many guns firing at me before! I dash inside as a bomb impacts against my hull. "Okay, Nelly, let's go!" I pull back on the steering wheel and up we climb over the building.

I aim a laser-guided bomb at the big, beautiful college below and obliterate the entire campus and surrounding area. Then, soaring over the nearby town, I destroy it as well. In my rage, I have killed a lot of Gettion for all the humans they butchered.

Many Gettion spacecraft circle around, trying to find and kill me. Too bad for them, I'm invisible. I shoot each of them down with ease.

"I declare war on Gettion for taking humans!"

If my country only knew I said that, they would probably kill me. But I don't care because to my country, Gettion don't exist anyway.

I reach Taylor's ship but see many other spaceships in pursuit.

"Taylor!" I shout over the radio, "We can't out run them."

He shouts back, "I say we turn around and fight to the death like human beings! What do you say?"

"I'm with you."

"I still can't believe this is happening," he mutters.

I maneuver Nelly beside their ship as the Gettion get closer. I see no way out for these vulnerable men and women. Death will come to them after all. I know that now.

Abruptly, the Gettion fleet halts in their tracks and back away.

"I guess I scared them away, Taylor! They did only have eighty warships and they know I'm a badass from Texas."

"You're probably right, Gunnar. I doubt that the massive warship behind us with its hundreds of fighters had anything to do with it."

I turn and see the Antonion mother ship. A calming voice tells us, "Please stop your engines and let us being you aboard."

Moments later, our crafts are safely pulled in.

Captain Mills approaches with a grin. "Yes, Gunnar I'm sure you just scared them off."

"Captain, can we get some clothes for these people, sir?"

He nods to a nearby officer who scurries off.

Soon, the humans, fully clothed, emerge.

"Sir, how did you know I needed your help way out here?" I ask.

"The Governor told me what you were doing by yourself."

"Sir, you've known that these aliens have been killing humans for years yet you allow it to continue."

"We and the Gettion are members of The Congress of Planets. If Earth were, too, humans would be protected. Until that day happens, there is nothing anyone can do legally about it."

"Can I join on Earth's behalf?"

"No, Gunnar. You are only one man, not a world power."

"Thank you, Captain, for helping us. I thought we were done for."

"Glad to help." He turns and departs for the bridge.

Taylor says to me, "I could use a cold beer right now."

"I know just the place. Follow me. Come on, Jennifer."

We go to the large bar Ed showed me before. The waitress arrives. "Two beers and one coffee, very hot, please," I tell her.

"How did you know I like my coffee that way?" Jennifer asks.

"That's how you ordered it last time we were here."

Taylor asks, "So we can go back home again, right?"

"Don't worry. You will go back home and see your family again. However, you won't remember any of this. If I see you downtown, you'll just walk on past without a second thought."

Jennifer tells me, "But I don't want to forget again. I feel horrible. Can you forgive me for what I said back at the restaurant? I'm sorry. That was no way to treat someone who saved my life. I want to know you better this time if you'll let me."

"You know," Taylor says, "I thought I was done for today—that no one could help me now. I was sure that death was waiting for me and then you show up."

"I actually came for Jennifer. The rest of you were a bonus."

Ed comes in. "Hey, buddy!"

"Ed! It's always good to see you again," I respond.

"You, too. Hi, Jennifer." She gives him a perplexed look. "So it's time to get them back home where they belong. Please follow me."

Jennifer says, "I want to go with Gunnar. Is that all right?"

I think for a moment. "Sure why not."

"One moment, please," Taylor says. "Gunnar, I don't know what to say but thank you for everything. I wish I didn't have to forget you. So long. It's been nice knowing both of you here in outer space."

"Bye, Taylor. One day maybe we will meet again. Who knows? You're a good fighter, and they really did run away because I'm a Texan, by the way."

Taylor smiles and goes off with Ed.

"Well, Jennifer, let me take you back home and put you to bed."

I pause and we give each other a funny look and chuckle.

Waiting at my time machine is Captain Mills. "You should know, Gunnar, that you are now a marked man. The Gettion want you dead after the destruction you caused on their planet. I'm glad you did what you did, though. Someone had to send them a message. Many humans died there and no one was doing a thing to help them. No one but you. I wish I could do more but my hands are tied. Good luck. You will always be welcome on my ship."

"I appreciate that, sir."

Jennifer and I hop in my time machine and take off. With all the enemies out there wanting to kill me, I put us in invisible-mode.

The journey back to Earth with Jennifer is all too short. We arrive at her home where she asks, "Want to come in and have something, like me?"

"Can I take a rain check on that? I'm a little beat right now."

"I'm a little tired, too. I will see you again, won't I, Gunnar?"

"Definitely."

I dash home and head straight to bed.

Chapter 10: **The Invasion**

In the morning, I get up and go down to find my brother, James, having a cup of coffee in the kitchen as usual.

"How's the time traveler man doing today," he asks.

"Not too good at the moment, brother."

"What's up?"

Debbie walks in with a big smile like always but abruptly stops. "What's the matter with you guys?"

James says, "I think my brother is either in love or in some kind of trouble. By the look on his face, it doesn't look like love."

"You know me too well, brother. If you must know I declared war on another planet and now they want me dead."

"You did not!" James shouts.

"Yeah, I did. And if I had to, I would do it again."

"Why?" Debbie asks.

"These aliens have been abducting many humans and performing experiments on them. If they needed a heart, they'd just take it out of one of us. They wouldn't care if the donor lived or died. I rescued a bunch of our people and destroyed the facilities on their planet. I put an end to it once and for all. I had no choice. It was either kill them or let them keep killing us."

"What are you going to do now?" James asks.

"I'll just live life like people do and see what happens. Today I'll go to the mall and look at the pretty women. That's my plan. See ya."

Arriving at the mall, I do my first lap and check out a few of the ladies. Still, I feel a bit on the cautious side.

Somebody taps my shoulder. I jump up and find my grandfather standing there. Seeing him is always an interesting experience. I think he has worked for the government a little too long if you ask me.

"What are you doing here, Gunnar?"

"Just girl-watching. You know me."

"If you had followed in your grandfather's footsteps and worked for the CIA, no one could ever come up behind you like that. Let's get some coffee and talk. It's not every day I get to see my grandson."

Seated at a doughnut shop, we chat for a spell.

"Gunnar, did you know that someone was following you?"

"Where?"

"Behind you. One has a brown suit and black shoes. The other has a light blue suit with brown shoes. Both have guns. Don't move. I'll watch them for you. I'm armed, too. You should keep your eyes open at all times. When I'm in other countries, I even sleep with a gun on. You never know when you'll need it."

"You don't' find it hard to sleep with a gun in your hand?"

"What you do is wrap it with rubber bands so it will be there when you need it. One time, an assassin snuck in while I was sleeping but I woke up and fell to the floor and fired two shots into him. That rubber band saved my life when there wasn't a second to spare. But don't you tell your grandmother about that!"

"I won't."

"I have to be going. Keep your eyes open, Gunnar. I can kill those men for you if you want and no one will ever know who did it."

"That's okay. I can take care of them myself."

"Suit yourself. Nice to see you again."

Watching my grandfather leave the doughnut shop, I observe the men standing by the stairs. I decide to exit the mall. They follow.

Approaching my truck, I push a button on my watch. Time slows to a standstill. I go to the men and take their guns. I also find throwing knives. I put the blades in my pocket with the bullets from their guns.

I return to where I was standing and press my watch again. Time returns to normal. I turn to them. They pull their guns and try to shoot. With no bullets, they look at me with surprise as I smile back. I take out their knives and throw one. The man on the right is struck in the heart and drops. I glare at the other and grin. He runs but does not get far from my other knife, which pierces his back. Bad day for them.

106

I kneel beside their bodies and note the "S" mark on their necks. They're Gettion. I have to stop this from going any farther.

In my truck, I call Debbie's superior, Charles Lewis, on my cell. "Charles, it's Gunnar. I can use your help."

"You name it and you got it."

"I need to speak with someone high up in the military; someone with the power to act at once. Our world may depend on it."

"I can give you a name and number, but you mustn't mention me. If this gets traced back to me, they might use their resources to find out more about you and learn of your 'you know what.'"

"No problem. He will never know about you or me."

Charles gives me the information.

"Thanks, Charles. By the way, how's Janet doing now?"

"She's doing a lot better now that she's home with her mother and father. She asks about you."

"You didn't tell her I'm the man who helped her, did you?"

"No, you told me not to."

"Tell her 'hello' for me the next time you see her."

"I will. So long, Gunnar."

I dial the number that Charles gave me. "Is this Philip Shelton?"

"It is. Who is this, please?"

"My name is Rodta. The people of my world will soon be taking over your Earth. I thought you should know this, Mr. Shelton."

"Is this some kind of joke? I'm not laughing."

"This is not a joke. If you hang up, your world will be lost along with your chance to do something about it."

"Assuming this is true, what do you want from me?"

"At the moment, nothing. We are already here on your planet. We have a mark on our necks shaped like an 'S.' Even our children do."

"This is ridiculous."

"Then tell me where you are. I'll let you see me in my spaceship. How is that for proof?"

"I'm in the lowest level of the White House."

"I will be there in a moment."

He laughs. "You'll never breach our security."

I hang up.

I press my ring and my time machine materializes. I climb inside. "Nelly, I want you to look like an alien spaceship. You hear me?"

I cross the country in mere seconds and penetrate the White House gate with ease, invisible to any eyes or cameras. I settle onto the front lawn and make my craft visible once more. Many men come charging out with guns, ordering me to get out.

A heavily armed group fires their rifles at old Nelly here but their bullets fall harmlessly to the grass. They try everything they can think of to open my door but cannot.

I then raise her up about five feet and hover there.

I see a man watching from within the White House. I phone Philip again and observe him answering his cell phone.

"Is this Rodta? Is that you outside our window right now?"

"Now do you believe me?"

"I think I might."

"In the parking lot of a mall in San Francisco are the corpses of two men from my world. They tried to kill me because I know of their plans. I killed them instead. As I said, you'll find an 'S'-shaped mark on their necks. Now you know what to look for. Some work for your Government right now and they are not your friends. They want you dead with everyone you know and love. I, however, am on your side. I must be going now but you will be hearing from me again, if they do not kill me first. So long. I hope I can call you my friend."

I make my time machine invisible and pass into the White House to overhear Phillip calling Charles Lewis in San Francisco.

"Charles, it's come to our attention that two dead men lay outside a mall in your jurisdiction. We have reason to believe that they have marks on their necks shaped like an 'S.' I'll need them recovered and for you to find out all you can about them. The safety of not just our country, but our entire world depends on it."

"I understand."

"Also, discreetly check the necks of any persons you send. If they have it, say nothing to them but report it directly to me."

"Yes, sir. I'm on it."

"And no one must touch those bodies but us. I want them guarded around the clock."

"I'll see to it, sir."

Charles hangs up and calls the police. After locating the bodies of the two men, he orders them to keep them under close guard until the FBI arrives. He then calls an Agent Jack Miller to his office.

"Close the door please and have a seat, Jack."

"What's the situation, sir?"

"I have known you a long time and know you are well acquainted with many others here at the office. I need you to handpick ten of your most trusted agents. I have an assignment for them but they first need to have a physical performed."

"Why is that necessary, sir?"

"To determine if they have a particular mark shaped like an 'S' on their necks. Only when they're clear will they be allowed on this case. And they must not be made aware of what we are really looking for."

"What does this mark mean?"

"What I am about to say must never leave this office. Turns out there are aliens from another world on this planet right now, possibly here in the ranks of the FBI. This mark is the only way to spot them."

"Seriously?"

"There are two bodies at the morgue with this same mark. Go and see firsthand."

Charles slowly draws his gun. A look of serious misgiving comes over Agent Miller's face.

"But before you go, I must ask to see your neck."

Miller looks in Charles's eyes and knows that he means business. With hesitation, he replies. "Yes, sir."

"Stand up please."

He cautiously inspects Miller's neck but finds nothing. "Go now." Charles holsters his weapon.

Miller hurries out, giving a look of misgiving.

Charles goes to his phone and dials.

At my home, I am just falling asleep when my cell rings.

"Gunnar, I need to talk to you right away."

"Charles? I'm in bed right now, can't it wait?"

"If you don't leave for my office right now I'll send two men to drag you here in your PJs!"

"All right! I'll be right there." I hang up on him.

I stagger into his office, yawning. "So what's important enough to lose my beauty sleep over?"

Charles gets up and shuts the door. Leaning against his desk, he glares at me and says, "I was speaking with Philip Shelton today."

"Oh, really?"

"Funny, I seem to recall giving a certain someone his number just this morning and now he's calling me up about two dead aliens in my local morgue. You wouldn't know anything about that, would you?"

I shrug.

"What the hell is going on here? I want the truth."

"Well, what happened was, I was at the mall where I was forced to defend myself against two alien assassins. I killed them before they killed me. There's nothing wrong with that, is there?"

"I need you to tell me all you know about these aliens."

"Where do I begin? Oh, yes. It all started in outer space. I was in this massive mother ship…" I went on to tell him the entire adventure. I told him about my beer with Bob the alien, who told me about the neck-mark and their plans to one day own the Earth. I explained the whole story with Jennifer, too. "Oh, yeah. And I almost forgot to tell you this part: I declared war on them."

"You did what?"

"But that was after I destroyed their medical college and its entire surrounding areas. Oh, and the best part is, I killed a whole lot of their doctors and students while doing that. It was a very good day for me. So anyway, now they want me dead, sir. That's it. No big deal."

"Maybe you should've consulted with us before you declared war on an advanced alien species! What were you thinking? And maybe you would think to bother telling us about it later?"

"Well, first of all, our government does not acknowledge that they even exist. And this job had to be done by someone and that someone was me. I had no choice but to do what I did."

"But why?"

"I'll tell you why. For a long time now, they have been abducting humans and butchering them for medical experiments. It had to stop. So I destroyed their facilities and put an end to it once and for all."

Jack Miller knocks at the door and enters. "Excuse me," he says.

"Finished with the physicals?" Charles asks.

"Yes, sir. Want me to come back?"

"It's because of Gunnar here that you're doing those tests at all. He knows more about what's going on than you and I put together."

"Two of the men had the mark. They did not act suspicious at all. Here are their names." He hands Charles a piece of paper.

"Thank you for your cooperation, Gunnar. Go back to bed and get some sleep," Charles says.

I go back home but can't sleep, so I watch some TV in the den.

There is a soft knocking at the front door.

It's Donna, who lives across the street. She gives me a few letters that were delivered to her house by mistake. She's very pretty. I really love her bright blue eyes. She has a marvelous face and smile that one does not forget easily. But she's only seventeen. A man can go to jail for doing what I'm thinking right now.

"Thanks," I tell her. She departs with a smile.

I wonder what kind of woman she'll grow up to be and if she'll look basically the same as she does now. Only time will tell. Actually, I do have a time machine! Why not see for myself?

I go outside and press my ring. My time machine appears. I jump in and go invisible to the world. I float across the street and then jump forward in time in short bursts so I can see her life changing in stages. I watch her on the porch in tight-fitting blue jeans. She looks really good in them. Now I see her with this guy.

I see nothing of her for a while. She looks a few years older and seems to be married to that same fellow. I believe she had moved out some time ago. I follow them to their new home.

Moving forward in time again, I see two boys with her now but no longer see her husband in the picture. Maybe they got divorced.

I stop. Thirty-five years have passed. Things look a lot different. I following her to work in my time machine and discover that she cuts hair for a living now.

I decide to get out and look around.

I walk into the salon and tell Donna I'd like a haircut.

"Sure, have a seat and I'll call you shortly."

I sit among several other customers and wait my turn. Eventually, she calls me into the back.

She sits me down and gives me a long, strange look. "Did you used to live across the street from me a long time ago?"

"Yeah, it's me, Donna, Gunnar Best."

"It can't be you, Gunnar. You haven't aged! You look the same as you did thirty years ago."

"Time changes people, but not me. You could say time belongs to me and is in my hands."

"What do you mean by that?"

"As incredible as it sounds, I have a time machine. I was curious about how you would end up and so I went thirty-five years into the future to see you. You're still the same pretty girl I used know across the street, just a little older is all."

"That does sound incredible, but here you are! How can I dispute it when see is believing? The truth is, though, I am not the same girl you knew. I married the wrong man and have been paying for it since. My mother tried to tell me but I wouldn't listen. Now look at me."

"If you want, I can change that for you. I can go back and tell you not to marry that man or something."

"No. If you do that, my two sons would not be born and I just love them too much."

"I understand. I won't do anything, then. You have my word."

"I always liked you, Gunnar, but was too young to say anything. Not anymore. We can do anything we want now. How about it?"

"I'd like that very much, but I must decline. You see, in my mind, you're still the same girl I used to know across the street and I want it to stay that way. If we were to do something, I'd feel like I should go to jail for it. You're still innocent in my eyes."

She looks a bit disappointed but I think she gets what I'm trying to say. She spends the next ten minutes cutting my hair. I can tell by her eyes that she's thinking of me. I know the eyes are the windows of the heart and soul of a woman. That's why I like to look into their eyes.

"You did a good job on my hair. How much do I owe you?"

"It's on the house for an old friend who lived across the street."

"It's been nice seeing you again, Donna, but I've got to go back."

"You, too, Gunnar, after all these years."

We step out into the waiting room. "Oh, there's one last thing I have to ask you, Donna. I'm just not sure how."

"Just tell me or I'll die wondering what it was."

I look upon all the people surrounding us. "Okay. Can I kiss you? And I don't mean a kiss on the forehead but on those beautiful lips of yours. That should cool me down for the next thirty-five years until I see you here again for my next kiss."

"Well, I am at work." She looks about. "But yes, I've wanted to kiss your lips for a long time too, so why not."

All eyes are on me and Donna. Holding her tightly, I give her the kiss that cannot be in my time. Part of me feels like a dirty old man, but who cares. I make sure it lasts a long time, since it has to last me thirty-five years before my next one. I let go of her and look into her eyes. Like me, I can see she is satisfied. "Good-bye, Donna."

She is speechless.

I walk out and press my ring. My time machine appears. I know I will always remember this day with Donna, the girl across the street. That kiss will live with me for a long time.

I arrive back home and find my brother and Debbie watching TV. James says, "The President's about to address the UN."

I sit down and watch the President approach the podium. He says, "Do not look upon me today as the President, but as a human being. For years, our government has denied the existence of extraterrestrial visitations. Now, however, we must admit the truth. It is my feeling that modern man has matured sufficiently to know this without panic. Yet, an alien race has come with plans of making our world their own. They must be stopped before it is too late. We must not wait until tomorrow, but must do something today. These aliens look just like us but have a mark on their necks, which resemble a letter 'S' as you can see on your TV screen. Should you find someone who has this mark, please contact the police at once and let them take care of it.

"Since these beings operate not just here in the United States, but across the world, we must work together to stop them. Any country that wants our help will receive it without question. Don't leave this problem to someone else. This is your world, too. Thank you."

"Well, that's it, then," James says. "The aliens have finally come. Did you know about this, Gunnar?"

"I did."

"Are you going to do anything about it?" Debbie asks.

"As a matter of fact, I was just about to visit Charles at the FBI."

"Can I come with you?" she asks.

"If you want. Let's take my pick-up."

Arriving at Charles's office, he says, "Although it's always good to see you again, Agent Alley, I never know if it's going to be good news or bad news with you and Gunnar."

"How many aliens do you have in jail right now?" I ask.

"Right now? Not one."

"How come?"

"Because whenever one is captured, all we have to do is turn our backs for a second and they're gone. What the hell is going on?"

"Their mother ship must be transferring them away. It's possible they realize now that their plans for taking over the Earth are finished and have begun recalling everyone stationed here—"

As I speak, an FBI agent bursts in and fires twelve rounds at me. His bullets, however, just bounce off. Others rush in and restrain him.

"What the hell?" Charles shouts. "No one has ever fired a weapon in this office before today!"

"I want his neck checked," I demand.

They find the distinct "S" mark.

The Gettion shouts, "You are a dead man! Maybe not today, but you can count on it, Gunnar! We will not stop until you are! Let go of me you bastards. I will kill you all, wait and see!"

"Take him away," Charles orders.

"They know I'm the one who got in the way of their plans," I say.

Charles tells me, "You know, Gunnar, you saved the world but the world will never know it—aside from us here in my office."

It then occurs to me that one beer saved our planet. It was that drink I had with the alien, Bob, that eventually lead to all this.

"How is it that you're not hurt?" he asks. "You should be dead."

"Don't worry about me, Charles. I am no more a space alien than you are. Let's go home, Debbie."

It's getting dark as we climb into my pick-up. I start up the engine and turn on my lights. "You know what?" I remark, "I think my left headlight is burnt out. I just had the right side replaced about a month ago. We'll have to stop by the auto place and have it replaced. It will just take them a few minutes to take care of it."

"Fine. Let's go."

Pulling into the service area, a man walks up and asks, "I take it you're here to replace that headlight?"

"You guys replaced my other one last month."

"My name is Randy and I'd be happy to help you, sir. Please park it over there."

After doing so, I climb out of my pickup and pop open the hood. Randy takes a look at my headlight. "There's a problem. Your battery is in the way of your headlight. See that?"

"You can take it out from the front grille. I saw the guy do that for the other headlight the last time I was here. Maybe we can ask him. Is anyone else here beside you?"

"I am the manager and I know everything about cars and trucks. What you're saying cannot be done by anyone here. If someone here attempted that, he was certainly in the wrong and won't be doing that again—not if I have anything to say about it."

"I did not come here to get anybody in trouble. On the contrary, he did a good job and that's why I came back to let him do it again."

"Well, he should have talked to me before he did that with your truck. His actions are why we're having this problem right now with you nice people here today."

"You're the only one with a problem here."

"I'm sorry you feel that way about it, sir."

"I'll go somewhere else for the light, then. I see you change oil. Can you at least do that for me now?"

"We have to wait an hour for the motor to cool down first."

"Randy, tell me the truth. You don't really know anything about cars or trucks do you?"

He pauses a moment. "It's true. I really know nothing about them at all. Why do you ask?"

"How did you get a job here?"

"Because I talk like I know what I'm talking about."

"Thank you for your time, Randy."

"Come again, sir."

At home, James asks, "So what's happening with the aliens?"

"They're leaving quickly enough. Our government is determined to boot them out from our country and the rest of the planet."

"Now that you've saved the world, what will you be doing next?" Debbie asks.

"After a good night's sleep, I was thinking of going to New York and looking around at all the women out there."

"Good night, then." James says.

Chapter 11: **The Plague**

In the morning, as James and Debbie get ready for work, I head outside and push my ring. "Hey, Nelly. How are you doing, old girl? Did you miss me?" Her doors start to open and I step inside. Nestled in the bucket seat, the doors start to close and I set the date for 2060 at high noon. "Let's go. The women of New York are waiting for us!" I pull the steering wheel back and we ascend into the air like a rocket.

Flying over the city of New York, I take us down near a bank. As I open the doors to my time machine, we remain invisible to all of the frozen people around us.

I get out and walk around to the trunk and look for my money in a box. There it is. Like Jack said, there's nothing better than gold when you need money fast. I grab one gold coin and head to the bank.

The time machine vanishes behind me as the people start to move again as though nothing had ever happened.

I walk into the bank and approach a teller window where a young lady greets me with a smile and asks, "Can I help you, sir?"

"I have this gold coin here. How much can I get for it?"

She inspects it and responds, I cannot say but "I'll be right back with someone who can." She soon returns with an older gentleman. "Hello, sir. The bank can only give you five thousand dollars for this. The price of gold is down now, I'm afraid. Do you want to wait?"

"No, five thousand will do just fine."

"Linda, here, will take care of your needs." He steps away.

She gives me my money and I am a happy man with five thousand dollars in my pocket. I feel quite rich.

"You're not from around here are you, sir?" she asks with a smile.

"No, I'm from California."

"I really shouldn't be asking this, but are you married, sir?"

"Never have been, but always looking for the right one. Why?"

"Do you have a girlfriend?"

No one at a bank has ever asked me such questions before. I look at her and say, "You can call me 'Gunnar' if you want to, pretty lady. And no, I don't have a girlfriend right now."

"I like you, Gunnar. We could go out and have a hell of a good time together. I can show you New York if it's your first time here."

Looking at her face, my eyes start to go down a little to her body. It all appears quite nice to me.

"I'm game. Let's do it. Whatever you want to do sounds good. Having a good time is why I came here."

"Great! I'm off in an hour. There's a restaurant across the street. Can I meet you there?"

"You got it, Linda."

Outside, I find a man parking a rather unusual car. "Nice car you got there. Does it run on gas?"

"No, no. Not this baby."

"How does it run, then?"

"I see you're not a car buff. Turning the key starts a small motor. It pulls in air from outside into an air tank and compresses it. In a few seconds, there's enough energy stored to kick in the big motor, which draws in a lot more air to power the car. It can go a hundred miles an hour if the police don't see me coming."

"Your car has no wheels?"

"I prefer RGP."

"RGP?"

"Reverse Gravity Pull. Keeps it above ground. Rides like a bullet! I like it about three feet up but teenagers like it lower at around three inches. They call it a 'low rider' but that's not my style. I'm not that young anymore. Know what I mean?"

"Well, you have an impressive car there, mister."

"Thank you, sir." He heads into the bank in a hurry.

Walking into the restaurant, I look around and wonder where all the people are. There should be a lot more out here in The Big Apple. I wonder what's going on.

I pass a nice-looking lady in a booth and we make eye contact.

I tell the man behind the counter that I'll have a cup of coffee.

Seated in a booth of my own, the man brings me my hot beverage. I ask him, "Where's the parade?"

"What parade are you talking about?"

"The one where all the people are."

"I don't know what you're talking about, sir."

"I thought New York had a lot of people in it."

"Did you just get out of prison or something? There is no parade. There won't be today or tomorrow. What you see is it. We did have a lot of people but that was forty-six years ago, young man."

"I ask, "What's your name, sir?"

"It's Roy if you must know."

"Roy, can you tell me what happened to them?"

"Well, it was a disease going around. It kept anyone from having children and that's why we have fewer people today."

That nice-looking lady in the booth gets up and walks over. "Can I buy you your coffee?" she asks with those big eyes of hers.

Roy shouts, "Sit back down or get the hell out of here, Elizabeth!"

"She leaves some money on the counter and walks by me saying, "I'll be seeing you again, big boy." She walks out with a sly grin.

"Why did you say that to her? She was really hot."

"All that woman wants is to get in your pants."

"Did it occur to you that maybe I want to get into hers, too? And what's wrong with her buying me my cup of coffee?"

"What's your name, big boy?"

"Gunnar. Gunnar Best."

"You don't get it do you, Gunnar? What did I just explain? Were you not listening? She has the disease. You'll get infected and the day of you having children will never come to be. It has spread worldwide and you don't want to catch it. It's not good for us single folk if you know what I mean."

"I was only thinking of a good time. So there's no cure, then?"

"Our government did discover one not too long ago. However, it only starts to work after six months of giving you the shot."

"Well, that's not so bad, I guess."

"The world wants that medicine real bad, but we won't give it out. Rumor is, the government feels that the country with the most people will be the strongest. So, that medicine is staying right here for now."

Linda from the bank enters. "Hi, Gunnar. Here I am as promised!"

"Thanks, Roy." Seeing her, he leaves us alone.

She sits in front of me and I can't help but look at her breasts and pretty face. She has a nice, small waist, too.

"Would you like a cup of coffee, Linda?"

"I would. They have the best coffee in town here. Bet you didn't know that, did you?"

"Roy, can I have another cup of coffee for this young lady?"

"You got it, Gunnar." He brings it with a big smile on his face as he looks at her. The smile she returns is much smaller.

"I could tell by how you talk that you were not from around here," she says nervously. Her face appears different somehow—something about her eyes has changed.

"I come from a small town in California that you never heard of before called El Sobrante."

"You're right, I never have heard of it. Is it pretty there?"

"Very pretty.

"You mentioned going out and having a good time?"

"Oh, sure! But you know, all we really need is our two bodies."

"But how do you know what kind of guy I am?"

"A woman can tell by the way a man talks to her and the way he looks at her, too."

I notice Roy watching us, listening to every word. I'm worried he might jump in and tell Linda to get the hell out of here, as well.

"Gunnar, I'm a thirty-two year-old virgin but want to be a mother one day. I want it to be with you. That's why I asked you here. I know men like sex more than women do. And you know I have a nice body. You know I can satisfy you sexually if you only let me."

"You were very honest with me, so I'll be very honest with you. Any man would love what you're offering. However, I must decline. Sex is one thing but a child is something else. One day, he or she may ask you, 'Where is my father? How did you meet him and how long were you together before he left us?' What will you say, then? 'After knowing him one hour, we had sex and then he left.' I'd want to be there when they throw their first ball and to talk to them later about boys and girls. That's a father's job. I love children too much to be a part of this. I hope you understand. You would have to marry me and I don't know you that well yet. So why don't we just hold off and see what our future holds for now?"

"You're right. I wasn't thinking about the child or love. I'm glad I met you first." She gets up and kisses me on the lips. "If you ever do want a family, you know where to find me." She goes to the door and stops. "Good-bye." Then, she is gone.

Roy comes over and says, "You are a very strong man. I believe her when she says she's a virgin. She eats here a lot and unlike other women, I have never heard her speak of being with another man. She just talks about her parents, so you know she's a good girl. If you had gone with her, I would not have stopped you. I'm sure she's clean."

"Thanks, Roy. What do I owe you?"

"It's on the house, Gunnar. I don't see many like you in here and I hope to see you again."

"Thanks." I wave and head out the door.

Walking down the street, this place feels like a ghost town. There are a lot of buildings but very few people in them. It's quite eerie.

I step into a store that has no customers. An eager woman asks, "Can I help you find something?"

"No, just looking." Seeing nothing of interest, I head out.

As I journey down the avenue, women stop and ask me to come home with them. One even offers to pay. Several are quite beautiful. Any man's dream. This town could be a lot of fun, but not for me.

Looking through the many windows, I see few people. The scope of what has happened begins to hit me. What can I do to help before it's too late for my county—that I love so much—and the world?

I approach a club with a large sign that says "DANCING tonight." Why not. A man at the door charges me fifty dollars to enter.

I go to the bar and order an ice-cold beer.

The guys here are wearing their pants high over their belly buttons and actually seem to think they look cool that way. In my time, guys liked to wear their pants down low like they just shit in their pants. Some are nearly to the floor while they hold them up with one hand. Even with their underwear showing as plain as day, they don't care because they think they're being cool. Why does everyone want to look exactly like everyone else? I'm in my black pants, cowboy shirt, brown leather jacket and black cowboy boots. Now that's me!

Compared to the rest of the city, this place has quite a few people. I notice that the guys are only dancing with the pretty women while the average ones are being ignored. I don't like this. I get up and walk passed the many-seated women watching me as I go by.

They move in like wild animals, trying to tempt me with their nice bodies. Ignoring them, I go to a short, heavy girl and ask, "Would you like to dance with me, young lady?"

Astonished, she responds, "Yes, I would love to."

I give her my hand and we dance. All eyes are now on us. Another woman comes over. She taps my shoulder and asks to cut in. I tell her, "If I do, some other man will go after this beautiful flower I have here in my arms and I may never get her back." A smile forms in the eyes of my dance partner and the other woman departs, disappointed.

When the music stops, I ask, "Would you like to sit with me? I'm here all alone tonight."

"I will because you ask me so nicely."

At our table, I ask, "What is your name?"

"Lisa. What's yours?"

"Gunnar."

"I never heard that name before."

"It means 'bold warrior.'"

The music starts. She asks, "Do you want to dance once more?" I can tell that she wants me. Her eyes give it away. That's why I love looking into a woman's eyes. They tell me everything I want to know. "You know, you're the only man in here who asked to dance with me. I guess I'm not pretty enough for the others."

"Who can say what's pretty? Can you or I? No, only the heart can. It's their loss. I know what I want and I have it—and that's you, Lisa. The outside of a woman fades away in time. But her inside stays the same if you really are a good person. And you are. A diamond is hard to find. But when you do, it makes you so happy. Your face is like a precious stone that shines inside of you and you are worth more than all those other women put together."

Grinning, she gives me her hand and I take her to the dance floor. Moving together, I feel her head against me as the music plays on. All the other girls watch, wondering what I see in her and not in them.

When the music stops, we go back to our table where the waitress asks us what we would like to drink.

I look at the waitress—who does look quite good—and tell her, "One beer for me and one cola for Lisa. I am right?"

"How did you know I drink cola?"

"I know my diamonds well."

When the waitress returns, I raise my beer and say, "To you, Lisa. May your life always be filled with joy."

Two other ladies arrive at our table. One of them says, "Hi, Lisa. Who's your friend?"

"Gunnar, these are two of my best friends, Helen and Jody."

I stand up and declare, "Any friend of Lisa's is a friend of mine. Would you ladies like to sit down with us for a drink?"

Helen says, "I'll just have a cola for right now."

"Me, too," says Jody as she looks at me with something peculiar on her mind.

"Waitress," I shout, "can we have two more colas please?"

Helen asks, "Where are you from, Gunnar?"

"California—the land of the free. If you lived there, you'd know what I'm talking about."

"What brought you to New York?"

"They say the women in New York are very easy on the eyes. It's true, too." The girls giggle.

"How did you get to be such a good dancer?" Jody asks.

"Don't tell anyone what I'm about to tell you, but an old friend of mine—whose name is Tom—his mom ran a dance class in our town and still does to this day. She said if we ever wanted a girlfriend, the first thing we had to do is learn to dance. She told us that women will actually come after us since most other guys don't like dancing at all."

"What's so bad about that?" Lisa asks.

"Well, during our lessons after school, one of us had to be the girl and other had to be the guy. When it was my turn, he'd always say, 'Gunnar, give me a kiss on the lips.' His mother told him that one day I really will. We danced fast and slow together. But if you asked Tom, he'd deny it ever happened. But ask his mother and she'll tell you."

Helen says, "I won't say anything."

"Me, neither," Jody adds.

"Lisa? You going to tell on me?"

"No, Gunnar, your secret's safe with me."

"Thank you."

"Gunnar?" Helen asks, "I don't want to be too forward, but will you dance with me?"

With a smile, I reach for her hand.

She's wearing a red dress that's a bit short but that's fine with me. Her sexy hair is longer than most women's, which is just the way I like it. Moving to the music, I can feel it with my arm around her.

126

"You smell nice," she comments. "You really know how to dress like a man; not like the other boys in here."

"Oh, thank you."

"Gunnar, I know it's not right for me to say this, but your lips just look so damn good to me. I want to kiss them so bad. I can taste them from here. And you have such large shoulders to hold on to while making love. I can bring out the fire in you if only let me. Can we go somewhere together? A real man like you doesn't really come around anymore in this town. I feel like this is my only chance."

"What about your friend, Lisa, over there? You would hurt her."

"She knows I'm more woman than she is. She would be too fat in bed to satisfy you anyway." She places my hand on her breast. It feels nice and firm. "There's more where that came from. Just imagine me without this dress. My body would be yours to do with as you wish."

The music stops. "Thank you for the dance. It was nice," I tell her. I go back to our table and she hesitantly follows.

Lisa says, "That sure was a lot more talking than when you were dancing with me."

"Yes, Helen was telling me about how pretty New York is.

"By the way, do any of you know of a good hotel?"

Jody says, "There's one right down the street. When you walk out, just turn right and go down two blocks. You can't miss it."

"Thanks."

As we talk, an angry man approaches and says, "You. Outside."

"What are you talking about? Do you work here?"

"You know what I'm talking about. I saw what you did to Helen with my two eyes. Don't deny it."

"That's easy to explain. Helen, tell him please for me."

"Ralph, you are not my boyfriend anymore and it's none of your business if I take someone's hand and put it on my breast. Get the hell out of here!"

He glares at me for a tense moment. He then turns and walks off.

Lisa asks her, "Why did you do that? You're my best friend."

127

"Yeah, but men like him never come around here anymore. You know that. What else could I do?"

I say to Lisa, "I have to get some sleep, but I do have time for one last dance. Shall we?" Reluctantly, she takes my hand and I walk her out to the dance floor. As I hold her in my arms, she begins to relax. Afterwards, I tell her, "Thank you, Lisa, for such a nice night."

"Wait. Here's my number. I hope you'll call me before you go."

I kiss her forehead and walk outside all alone in the night.

Arriving at the hotel, I approach the counter where I'm greeted by a friendly, older gentleman.

"One room, please with a window to look out to the city," I say.

After I pay him, he instructs the bellhop to take me to room 910.

Once there, we enter and he opens the window to let in some air. He faces me, expecting a tip. "Here you are, my good man," I say.

"Thank you, sir." He departs.

I take my jacket off and drape it over a chair before lying on the bed and closing my eyes for a short while.

There is a knock at the door. I get up and find Helen there. "What are you doing here?"

"Can I come in?"

"Have a seat." She does so with a gorgeous smile and her perfect body to go with it. "Everything okay?"

"Make love to me. Lisa is not here and never has to know about it. You do like my body, don't you?"

"I do, but I don't know if we should." As I speak, she slowly takes off her clothes, starting with her blouse, which falls to the floor. Next goes her bra. I can only stare, speechless, as her skirt drops next. The best part, her panties, goes last.

"Come to me, Gunnar. Now take your clothes off, too."

A man can be weak in such moments. I start removing my clothes. Naked as a newborn baby, I put my arms around her and kiss her lips while cupping and massaging those breasts I do love so very much.

128

"Please don't stop," she says, staring at my hand on her breast. "You do that so well. Don't say this is the first time you've done this. I have never felt like this before. Just tell me what you want and I'll do it. I'll do anything. Just ask me."

"Protection comes first." With that out of the way, I grab her waist and pull her close, pressing her breasts against my chest. Laying her softly onto the bed, I start kissing her neck while on top of her and we make love for some time.

"Oh, Gunnar! You feel so good inside me. You're the best lover I ever had. Please don't stop. Please don't..." She climaxes.

I position her on top of me this time and put my hands on her hips as she moves faster and faster until climaxing a second time. "You're killing me, Gunnar!" She finally stops and lies next to me for a while. "What a ride you gave me!"

"Why don't we get some coffee downstairs," I suggest.

"Just give me a minute to recover."

Eventually, we put our clothes back on. She kisses me and says, "Let's come back after and do it again."

I hear a creak at the door. I open it to find Lisa. Her grin instantly turns to dread at the sight of Helen. "What's she doing here?"

"She just wanted me to know that you liked me and to make sure I called you before I went back home." Lisa gives me a skeptical look. "You don't believe me?"

After a lengthy pause she says, "Yes, I believe you. For a second, though, I thought you were having sex with my best friend."

"We just met two hours ago. What kind of guy do you think I am? I only have eyes for you, Lisa. You know that."

"I'm sorry for not believing you."

I feel awful for lying, but I think it would be far worse for her to hear the truth.

"So why are you here?" I inquire.

"I wanted to know how long you were in town so maybe we could do something."

"Tell you what; let's all go down now and have a cup of coffee."

"Okay," she says.

We make our way to the restaurant downstairs where the waitress shows us to a nice table and I order us three cups of coffee.

"So what do you two think about this thing with men and women not being able to have children?" I ask.

"It's really sad," Lisa replies.

"I hear our government has a medicine to stop the disease," I say.

"Yeah," Helen responds, "but it takes six months before it works. It first has to kill the disease and then it takes time to clean out."

Lisa adds, "Tomorrow at city hall, the doctor who developed it is giving a talk, along with someone from the armed forces."

"Why does the military have to say anything?" I ask.

"They need men in the military," says Lisa. "So if you're sixteen, they want you and there's a lot of pressure being put on parents to get them in, even though the kids aren't so excited about it. They'd rather stay at home with their parents and go to school, but the military tells them they're men now and that the schools are better in the military."

Helen adds, "That's why if you break the law now, you don't go to prison anymore. You're put in the military."

Lisa says, "Sometimes a recruiter just sees a boy on the street and asks his name. Next day, the recruiter shows up at his home and says, 'Your son's in the military now. It's the law. Boy, get your clothes. You're coming with us.' They have that option in certain cases."

"Unless you work in government," says Helen. "Their sons never have to go. For everyone else, though, it's the military or get arrested, which is really the same thing to me. That's the law for you."

I ask, "What time is that talk tomorrow?"

"I think ten o'clock," says Lisa.

"I have to be there, which means I need my sleep so I must leave you ladies now. I'll be in touch tomorrow."

They appear disappointed and a bit confused, but seem okay about it as I pay the bill and head upstairs to my room, alone.

Come morning, I get ready for my day and push my ring. My time machine appears here in my room. I take it to city hall, before the talk is to begin. Invisible to everyone, I watch them gather in a huge room. Before I open my door, I press a button that makes my craft visible. I step out and close my door.

Astonished, a man asks, "How did you and that thing get in here?"

The rest of the people soon focus upon me.

An Army lieutenant yells, "Who the hell are you?"

"I have come to speak! The world depends on you and me, today and tomorrow, before it is all lost for good. Let me help you." To the military officer I cry, "You don't need boys in the military, but men. I can give you all the men you want and more."

A man barks, "Would someone please get this clown out of here?"

I say to him, "If you want your epidemic stopped once and for all, I can accomplish that much more swiftly and effectively than you can. By tomorrow, it will be gone for good; never to return. Arrest me and it will continue and never stop. It's your choice."

"How can you stop it?" a woman asks.

"With this machine here."

"What is it?"

"A time machine!" I respond.

A rumbling of chuckles and groans move through the room.

"With it, I can go back in time or into the future. I live in the past with my brother and we do not have this sickness and there are many people here in New York then."

A woman steps in from another room and asks, "Shall we begin?"

"Not yet," a young gentleman tells her. "So how can you stop this disease from happening, sir?"

"With your medicine, I can go back in time and give it to the first who are infected. If you wish, one of you can come with me."

"Why are we even listening to this guy?" someone shouts.

The lieutenant says, "He may be telling the truth. How else could he get in here with that thing without us seeing?"

An Asian man yells, "I am with the Center for Disease Control. I will go with him and ensure our medicine does not fall into negative hands. I know where to go and when." He walks to me, looks into my eyes and asks, "What's your name, sir?"

"Gunnar Best."

"I am Lee Whan. When I first heard of this disease, I prayed for a miracle. I want to know if you are that answer to my prayer."

"Could be, Mr. Lee Whan. Only time will tell."

The Lieutenant makes his way through the crowd and mutters to me, "If this machine of yours is the real deal, we can pay you—"

"It's not for sale, sir, and never will be at any price no matter what you offer me."

"Lee," I state, "this time you are going to will be only temporary. Do you understand? I don't want to hear that you want to stay there longer, like so many others who have traveled with me."

"I agree to do as you say, Mr. Best. This is my home."

We look into each other's eyes and both understood each other.

"Then let's go to the past."

"One moment, please." As Lee gets the medicine, the Lieutenant softly asks, "Is there any way I can go with you two?"

"I'm afraid there's no room, sir."

Lee returns. I place my hand on his shoulder and open the doors. Time stops all around us.

"What happened?"

"That's just the way the time machine works. They will return to normal after I close the doors."

Astonished, he climbs in with me.

"How far back are we going?"

"The disease began its travel around the world in the year 2020. That's where we'll start tracking its source."

I engage my time machine and hurl us back into the past.

"Now what?"

"Now we need to go to the Center for Disease Control office up ahead where I work—or I guess, will work in the future."

Lee gazes upon his building and comments, "How time changes things. In my time, this is a much older building."

"No one can see us. Where do you want to go?"

"Up ahead is the entrance but there is a fence."

"There are no fences I cannot pass through. Watch this." I go right through and take us down in front of the building. We both get out and everybody stops moving. Our doors close behind us and all the people go back to normal. We walk on in. At the front desk is a young lady receptionist. She is very pretty.

"My name is Lee Whan and I need to speak to Douglass Hunter."

"One moment please." She makes a brief call. "Dr. Hunter is too busy to see anyone right now and asks that you make an appointment for next week sometime."

"Young lady, you tell Mr. Hunter I need to see him right now. Not tomorrow or next week. You tell him I know where he lives on Mary Street and when I leave here, I'm going to tell his wife about a certain lady friend of his. I'll give him one minute before I go."

I like this guy's style.

Less than a minute later, Mr. Hunter walks briskly out toward us. "You wanted to see me?"

"Yes," Lee says. "Shall we talk out here in front of her or in your office where it's more private?"

"Please follow me," he says with a forced smile.

We arrive at his office and he shuts the door quite hard. "So, how much money do you bloodsuckers want from me?"

"We don't want any money from you," I respond.

Lee tells him, "I'd never say anything to your wife, Doug. You don't realize this, but I'm your best friend."

"What are you talking about? I never saw you before today and you know it, so don't come out here with that bullshit. We both know what you are here for so just tell me how much!"

133

"I know about you and the women in your life because you told me about them a long time ago, in the future.

"I'd love to play this game all day but I've got too much work."

"Doug, me and my friend here come from the year 2060 and this sterilization disease has gotten way out of control there. We must do something to stop it here and now before it's too late. You and I are friends there in the future."

Doug tells us, "We believe that this disease you are talking about will die out in the near future, Mr. Whan."

"Before, Doug, you always called me Lee. It's kind of nice to hear you call me Mr. Whan for the first time."

I tell Doug, "If this disease is not stopped now, it will ravage the world like you won't believe. If you were to come to New York in the future as I did, you will see how desolate this planet has become with so many never to be born."

Lee explains, "In this box is the medicine you need to stop this. It takes six months to kill the virus and thoroughly clean the body of the illness. After that, the person will regain the ability to reproduce."

Doug looks at me and asks, "What's your name?"

"My name is Gunnar."

"So you live in the future, too, I presume?"

"No, I come from your past. 2011."

Lee tells him, "In the future, you are my boss here at the CDC."

"This is all a bit tough to swallow."

"Gunnar and I must go back home to the future, Doug. We did our job and I hope things will be a lot better there than when we left it. You'll be able to replicate plenty more of the medicine from that."

"Lee," Doug says, "if what you are saying is true, why don't you just stay and work with us? You know this disease better than anyone here and know what else is coming down the road."

Lee looks at me and says, "I already promised I wouldn't."

Doug turns to me. "Why?"

"This happens every time! I go visit a place, see a problem and try to help, then someone wants to stay in another time. But it's wrong to leave people in a time they do not belong because it alters the time line unnecessarily. Now, I just tell them from the start that they have to go back home and that's it. Time is in my hands, so I am the one who makes the decisions here."

"But Gunnar," Doug pleads, "he understands the disease far better than anyone here. You want people to lose their lives in our country and across the world because of you?"

"Of course not. But his actions could also change things in a way which prevent as many other people from being born as this disease."

"But—"

"I could make it so he and I never came back and you'd now have no medicine at all. How about that?"

He thinks for second. "Okay, you got me."

"Lee, if you want to stay you'll never return to the future without waiting a long time for it. This will be your home and your loved ones will never see you again. In the future, nobody will ever know what happened to you. You'll just be gone, if that's what you want."

"My girlfriend and I were planning on getting married someday. Kind of hard to do that from here. Let's leave the past in the past."

"Let's go back home, then."

Doug says, "Good-bye, Mr. Whan. If you're right, I'll see you in the future. Gunnar, you're the first time traveler I have met so far. I'm glad it was you since you can out-talk me so well. So long."

As I shake his hand I mention, "For the sake of what people think of your sanity and career, you might want to keep all this to yourself."

"Definitely, I will."

Lee and I exit. I press my ring and my time machine appears. We climb inside and the doors start to close. Seconds later, we arrive at City Hall at the same time we originally left. "Oh my god!" Lee says, "There are people all over the place!" None of them, however, are the same people that were here when our trip began.

We glide over to the CDC building and set down. We get out and enter the offices where a man says to Lee, "Where have you been, Mr. Whan? We've been looking all over for you."

"Mr. Whan," I say, "it is time for me to go. Have some fun now. Like I said to Doug, best to keep all this to yourself."

"You know, you saved our world and it'll never know about you. I say to you, then, thanks for saving us, Gunnar."

"Farewell, my friend."

I shake his hand and walk away. Outside, I push my ring and there my time machine reappears. Her doors open and I enter.

I go to the bank to see Linda one more time. I go in and approach her and say, "You look so very pretty today, young lady."

She responds, "I'm a married woman. Do you have some business here? If not, please leave."

"I am very happy to know you are married, Linda. I will go now."

She looks at me oddly as I turn and leave the bank.

Walking outside, I look around and say, "Good-bye, New York. And you're welcome. Don't mention it. Nelly, it is time to go back home to the year 2011 where I belong. Let's go."

Chapter 12: **Remembering The Alamo**

From the skies of New York I travel back home to the West Coast and the year 2012.

It's late afternoon as I set down in my time machine's very own parking spot in one corner of my backyard.

Stepping into my house, I find James and Debbie in the kitchen. She looks at me as I enter and abruptly asks, "Where were you born?"

"Hello to you, too," I respond.

"I've been meaning to ask for a long time but keep forgetting."

"Well, if you must know, I was born in Texas. Specifically, in San Antonia near that place where the Alamo fought to free Texas from Mexico. A lot of good men died there on both sides. And in the end, no one really won that war and no one ever will."

Debbie asks, "What do you mean by that? I thought we won that fight for Texas."

"Debbie, Debbie... Can ancient Rome say it won Rome? Nobody can say that because they are all dead, yet Rome it still there. No one owns Rome or Texas. Only time will tell who will own it next."

"Give me a break," James mutters.

"Speaking of Texas," I continue, "I'd give anything to be there with Davy Crockett and his men, fighting at the Alamo. Wouldn't it be great to see him and talk to him and be there and see it happening right before your own eyes?"

"Why don't you just go, then," James says. "You've got a time machine for Christ's sake. What's stopping you?"

"Sounds like the last place I'd ever want to be," Debbie remarks.

"I will! But first I've got to get some money."

"Where are you going to get that?" Debbie asks.

"Don't forget that you work for the FBI. You don't want to know, so don't ask."

"You're right. Don't tell me."

"I'm off, then!"

"But you just got here from New York!" Debbie says.

"Texas waits for no man! Texas wants me now!"

"Again," James points out, "you have a time machine, you moron! What difference does it make when you leave?"

"Nonsense!" I respond. "I can hear Texas calling to me. I must go now and fight for her and say good-bye to Davy Crockett!"

James groans. Debbie wears a crooked smile.

I rush out of the house, pressing my ring two times and bringing my time machine back to me. It rises several inches from the ground as its doors open. Stepping in, I sit within my bucket seat and set the controls for April 5th, 1980 at 2:00 pm.

I pull on the steering wheel and we rise up to the sky. Time begins rolling back. A few buildings come and go. I now see my destination. I take Nelly down next to a large building. The city stops frozen as I open the doors and get out, only to resume when I'm clear.

I enter the office building where a lady behind the front desk asks, "Can I help you, sir?"

"Yes, I want to buy some stock."

"I will call a stockbroker to help you."

A man comes out of an office. He looks me over, as if to establish my financial worth. "My name Calvin. And you are?"

"My name is Gunnar Best."

"And you want to buy some stock? You came to the right place. Step into my office please and have a seat."

It's a pretty fancy office, I must say.

"Coffee?"

"I'm okay, thanks."

"Is there a particular stock you have in mind, Mr. Best?"

"Yes, it's called Steve's Electronics."

"Did you say 'Steve's Electronics'?"

"Yes, why?"

"Well, I can tell you right now that this stock is no good. You'll lose your shirt on it. Take my word on that, Mr. Best. But I can show you some great stock that can make you a lot of money in the future."

"I know the future a lot better than you do, Calvin, and that's why I'm buying this. If you do not want to trade this for me, maybe you know someone else who will?"

"Fair enough. But remember that I warned you. How many shares do you wish to buy?"

"How much a share?"

"About two dollars. How many do you want?"

"A thousand."

"Okay, but can I just say something here? It might not be right to tell you this but I feel I must."

"What's on your mind?"

"You seem like a good man, but I think you're crazy!"

"Oh?"

"How would you like to pay?"

"Cash." From a bag, I count out two thousand dollars for the man. "Can I come back next week on Monday for my certificates?"

"Yes, no problem. I will see you Monday, then, sir."

I go outside and press my ring two times, calling my time machine back into existence. I climb in and punch a few keys on the dashboard computer, hurling us through time to Monday.

I climb back out and return inside the building to find that same young lady at the reception desk.

"I'm here to see Calvin if I may."

Calvin comes out of his office. "Hello there, Mr. Best. Come on in and have a seat. If you want, I can exchange your stock for something better while there's still time."

"No, sir. I'm happy with what I've got."

"Well, then, here is your stock."

"Sir," I tell him, "you are a good man for trying to help me. Thank you for that. Here is five-hundred dollars for you. But I do know the future, so if I were you, I'd put that on the same stock I did and you will get a lot more money than that five-hundred. Good day."

Astonished, he stares at the money in his hand as I leave.

I return to my time machine and program a new destination for us. Pulling back on my steering wheel, I say good-bye to 1980 and move forward. Things begin to change once more but I'm getting used to it.

I locate another building and put us down in front.

I disembark from my craft and she vanishes behind me.

Inside the office is another young woman behind a reception desk. "I'd like to sell some of my stock I have here, please."

"Yes, sir. I will get someone to help you." She picks up her phone and soon an older gentleman steps out of his office."

"Can I help you, young man?"

"Yes, I hope so. I want to sell my stock here."

"Please come in my office and take a seat. What's your name?"

"Gunnar Best."

"I'm George. Can I see your stock certificates, Mr. Best?"

Looking them over he says, "Steve's Electronics? You know, this stock is very hot right now. You sure you want to sell? I wouldn't if I were you. The price is going up and up as we speak. Wait a while and you'll make a lot more."

"How much is it going for right now?"

"About a hundred bucks a share."

"George, I have one thousand shares and I want to sell them all."

"Very well. It's your stock and your money. You'll get about one-hundred-thousand dollars."

"Can you transfer it directly to my bank account?"

"Yes, if you're really sure you want to do this."

"I'm sure. It's only money; not life or death."

After our transaction is complete, he says to me, "Well it's been nice knowing you, Mr. Best. I hope we can do business again."

"Count on it."

I walk out to my time machine and get in. I know just where to go. I see the place all the time whenever I go to the restaurant. "Let's go, Nelly!" I pull back on my steering wheel and up we go.

Arriving at our destination, I take us down. "Easy does it now, old girl." After a skillful landing, I step out and enter a small store as my craft vanishes behind me.

"Help you find something?" a bearded man asks.

"I hope so. I need pants, a shirt and shoes, all made of buckskin."

"You know, I get I got of people in here for that same thing until I tell them how much it's going to cost. Then they say 'No, thank you' and march right on out of here."

"Is that right?"

"And so before I tell you how much it's going to cost you, do you want to sit down first?"

"No, I can take it standing up."

"Around one-thousand dollars."

"I thought you were going to scare me with something outrageous. I can give you a thousand and get rid of the scared part, how's that?"

The man looks pleasantly surprised.

"The thing is, I need it to look old. If you have some like that, I'll still give you a thousand for it."

"All my supply is new. But I did know a man who died about two years ago. I think his wife still has his buckskins. He was a bit bigger and fatter than you, but if she'll go for it, I can make it fit you."

"Would someone, let's say, at the Alamo in the early 1800s still think it was all from their time?"

"Davy Crockett himself would not know the difference. You see, I do a lot of work for Hollywood and they want their outfits to look as authentic as possible. I do it the same way as my great grandfather did for real before he passed away."

"I think we got a deal. I'll pay the woman anything she wants for the buckskins, but this has to stay between you and me. Understand?"

"You got it. Come back around this time on Saturday and I'll tell you if I got 'em for you."

"By the way, what's your name?"

"It's Davy. Like Davy Crockett."

"Until we will meet again on Saturday, Davy..."

I head out to my time machine and press my ring twice. Looking back through the store window, I can see Davy frozen in time. Little does he know that I am a time traveler and that soon I'll be with the real Davy Crockett himself. What he wouldn't give, I'm sure, to be in my buckskin shoes. My door starts to open and I go inside my craft. I push a few buttons and flip a few switches and in a blink, it's already Saturday. I put on a different shirt and go out and into the store again. There, I see Davy talking to a woman as I approach. Recognizing me, he says, "Gunnar, I want you to meet Lisa Scott, the lady I spoke of."

"I'm so sorry for your loss," I express to her.

"Thanks. It was a sad day when my husband died but that was two years ago. Davy says you want to buy his old buckskin clothing?"

"That's correct."

"I wanted to meet the man who would be wearing my husband's prized possessions. I think we would have liked you and would have been fine with this. He was an outdoorsman you know; like you."

"How much do you want for them?"

"How about two-hundred dollars. Does that sound fair?"

"No, it does not." All eyes in the store are on me. She and Davy stare at me, speechless. "Let me tell you what I think is fair. I'll give you one-thousand dollars. How does that sound to you, Mrs. Scott?"

A sigh of relief moves through the room.

"Yes, that sounds fair to me, Mr. Best. You're a good man."

I pull the money in cash and count out one-thousand dollars into her palm. "Thank you so much. May God keep you safe."

"No, it should be me thanking you. Your husband's buckskins are worth a lot more to me than money."

"I have to go now," she says with a tear in her eye as she leaves.

Davy says, "That was a real nice thing you did, there. Now let's take some measurements. You want boots, too, don't you?"

"Yes, thanks."

After my measurements are taken, he says, "I should have all this ready for you in three weeks—on the twenty-second."

"Oh, yeah. I'm also going to need a large holster for my flintlock musket and a good saddlebag for my belongings and a smaller leather bag for carrying other stuff, too."

"I'll see what I can come up with."

"Fine. I'll see you in three weeks, then."

I go outside to my time machine and skip ahead once more to the twenty-second. Returning back into the store, after just a few minutes, I find Davy greeting me with a proud smile.

"I'm all done with your clothes, boots and holster. I made them all out of buckskin, including a big and small bag for your belongings."

"They look great!"

"Why don't you go into our dressing room over yonder and see if everything fits you. And don't forget the boots."

I try them on, only to find them a bit too big.

Davy explains, "No, that's just right for you, Gunnar. You see, if too small and tight, things would get too hot. Being big lets the air in. Trust me, you'll thank me for this one day."

"I'll thank you now for all your help. Here's another thousand for you and your time." I shake his grateful hand and depart.

Out on the road again, I head for a nearby gun store where I know they'll have any gun I want, even a musket. Climbing out, my door closes behind me and Nelly is gone. I walk into the store and locate a man who works there.

"Can I help you?"

"I hope you can. I'm looking for a flintlock rifle."

"One sec," he says as he heads behind the counter. "Here we are."

"It looks very nice," I tell him, "but I don't know anything about muskets. In fact, this is the first one I've ever held."

"Sir, are you here just to talk about flintlock muskets or are you here to buy one? I'd like to know before we go any farther."

"I just—"

"This is not a cheap item and not something a person who knows nothing about them just runs out a buys for no reason."

"Sir, you got me all wrong. I do want to buy a flintlock musket. But I can go somewhere else if you have a problem with me."

"You should know that this weapon you're looking at costs six-thousand dollars."

"That's it? Go on, then. Tell me more about it."

He seems to lighten up a little. "It's a nice gun. You'd be proud to own it. Let me show you this. It has a little box here at the end."

"What's it for?"

"Anything you want. Most use it to hold grease or cloth patches."

"Huh?"

He groans. "They're used to insert your bullet more easily into the rifle bore, holding it tightly in the barrel."

"Oh, right."

"It is, however, multi-purpose. It also holds any small articles like spare flints or caps or small tools. The wood is maple and has a long rectangular door at the end here."

"Never seen anything like this."

"They're not common. See the carving here in the stock? This has silver inlay-work that was done here. What more can a man ask for?"

"Out of all your flintlock muskets, if you were buying it yourself, which one you would choose?"

"Wait right here," he says as he goes somewhere in the back area. He returns with a gun wrapped in cloth, which he carefully removes. It sure does look pretty. "This is the one for me."

"And why do you say that?"

"I know you don't know much about muskets, but this one was very well made. It's well balanced, too. Hold it like you were going to shoot." I press it against my shoulder. "How does it feel?"

"It feels real good in my hands."

"Now try this first one again and tell me which you like best."

"No comparison."

"You know, sometimes there's one gun in a million out from the factory that's perfect. I believe this is that gun. I just love this baby."

"Then I guess, the number one question is, how much is it?"

"I'm not going to lie to you, sir. This is worth thirty-thousand."

"I see you have a shooting range out back. Can I try it and see if I like it? I will buy it today if I do."

"Barry! Come watch the counter for a few minutes." He takes me downstairs to a large room with targets at the far end. He shows me how to load the round bullet and place a bit of black powder onto the side of the gun. "Before you fire, pull back the hammer. It has a flint stone in it, which strikes the metal, creating a spark which ignites the powder and sends the bullet out of the gun. Understand?"

"Yep."

"Now you can shoot at that target over there."

I take aim and squeeze the trigger. I nail the target in the middle!

"That's good shooting for the first time with a flintlock."

"It feels real good in my hands. If I buy it, what comes with it?"

"What do you mean?"

"I'm saying if I plunk down thirty-thousand dollars and you have nothing free to throw in, maybe I should go someplace else and see what they have to offer."

"What did you have in mind?"

"How about a couple of those horns that hold powder and some bullets—about two hundreds of them—and we got a deal here."

"Let's go upstairs and do the paperwork."

"Oh yeah, I'll need a good flintlock pistol, too."

"I'll just cut to the chase and show you the best pistol we carry. It costs one thousand dollars but I know you'll like it. One minute." He returns with a gleaming firearm. "A thing of beauty, don't you think?"

"Yes, it is. Can I fire it?"

"Be my guest. You load it like the musket."

He shows me how and I fire off a round.

"Another fine shot!" he shouts.

"Yes, I'll take this, too."

As we go upstairs he asks, "How do you want to pay for all this?"

"With my debit card, please."

He takes my card and conducts the transaction. "It went through just fine. The musket is yours. Take care of it and your new pistol."

"I will. Like my life depends on it."

"Where are you planning on going with them, if I may ask?"

"I'm going to the Alamo to fight side-by-side with Davy Crockett and Jim Bowie."

He gives me a funny look, like I've lost my marbles.

"Okay, then. Have a good time at the Alamo and say "Hi" to Davy Crockett and Jim Bowie for me."

"I will. Thanks for the help. I'll be back one day if I'm not killed."

I next go to a survivalist store down the street and buy a big bowie knife, a blanket, matches, toilet paper, a towel and some jerky.

Returning to my time machine, I lift my hand and press my ring two times. There's my sweet girl ready to do her magic. I climb inside and settle into my bucket seat. "Nelly, you don't know where we're going, but I'll tell you, old girl. We are going to San Antonio, Texas, where the Alamo is. I'll be fighting there with Davy Crockett and Jim Bowie. You know, before, I only read about them but today, because of you, I'll actually get to go there and know them in person."

I set the date for the first day of March, 1836. The time, about five P.M. I hit the green button. Grabbing hold of the steering wheel, I pull back and we begin our ascent. Onward to San Antonio, Texas where I was born. There's no stopping me now. When a man like me makes up his mind, there's just no changing it.

146

Chapter 13: **San Antonio, 1836**

Buildings come and go before my eyes as time changes outside of my window until I finally arrive at our destination. My time machine slows until stopping on the ground in front of a small cantina.

Here I am, in 1836 at the time of the Alamo.

"Thank you, old girl. That's why I like you so much; because you do what I want you to do, unlike other women out there."

My door opens. I go outside and look around at this time period. It looks a lot different from when I was last here in 2012. There are no pretty buildings standing, no pretty grass on the ground and no pretty women walking by in short dresses. Just me on a dirt road with these old buildings that need a good paint job. How time changes things.

No one can see me on this cold night except the stars. The people around me remain frozen as I change clothes on the street. "Keep your eyes closed, old girl. No peeking." Putting on my buckskin clothes, I keep one eye on Nelly, who is a lady. I place my raccoon hat on my head, sling on my cow horn full of gunpowder and load up on round bullets. And I mustn't forget my salt and pepper, which I stick in my small bag. Lastly, my blanket and toilet paper go into my big bag, too.

"Well, Texas, here I am; ready to fight at the Alamo!"

But first, I must go to my trunk and get out some money I can use here as well as some good old-fashioned gold.

Finally, I press my ring and my time machine vanishes.

"Good-bye, old girl. I will see you later. You know I love you. It's just you and me now, Texas, and there's no turning back now.

As I walk down the dusty street, I smell something. Manure. It's all over the damn place. I guess I better get used to it again. Watching where I step, I make my way down the street.

I see a sign that reads, "Room for Rent." It's not a big hotel or anything, but what the hell. I walk in and find a man behind the front desk. He's very skinny with a large Adam's apple.

"Need a room, mister?" he asks.

I can't help but note his Adam's apple moving up and down as he talks but I try not to stare or laugh. In his white shirt and brown vest, he looks like a nerd to me with his hair parted down the middle.

"I do," I respond.

"I'll show you to it, then."

He swings open a door and steps in. I count six beds.

"You'll have to share with five others. This ain't the big city here, mister. You know that, don't ya?"

"Yep, I do. What do I owe you for these beautiful quarters?"

"Half dollar a night."

"I'll take it."

I set my bag down and look him in the eye. "I'll be going out now. If anything goes missing from this bag, when I get back, you will lose one little finger. You understand?"

Knowing I mean business, his Adam's apple jolts up and down as his eyes lock onto the knife at my side. "This blade has killed a lot of men in its time." I pull it out. "It cuts real good."

"I get your drift, mister."

I turn, walk outside and head back toward the cantina. It reads, "Bexar Cantina." That's right... Bexar was the name of San Antonio before it was called San Antonio.

With a lot of noise coming from inside, it seems like a good place to have a good time and get to know the people out here in Texas in this time in the past.

Going in, I see a lot of tables, just like in the movies. But this isn't the movies. It's real life. The place is packed. Some are dancing while others are kissing the women. I go to the bar, walking very slowly and watching everybody. I seat myself and tell the man behind the bar that I'll have a bottle of Tennessee whiskey and one glass.

"That'll be three dollars." He gives me a skeptical look. I go to the small bag on my belt and take out three dollars and put it down. I then give him a look. He's a bit chubby but still looks mean; like a man that could kill you just by looking at you. His face has a lot of cuts.

I take my bottle and go to a table next to a wall and have a seat. I look around before I open it and then pour a little in to my glass to clean it and begin to drink in peace.

Two men approach in buckskin shirts, pants and boots. They have beards and long hair. One has a big cut on his face. I'd say they were outdoorsmen. They carry knives about ten inches long and don't look friendly. One of them says, "Me and Steve here were watching you from by that window. He said you look Mexican. But to me, you look like one of us white men who has just been out in the sun too long."

"And you are?" I ask.

"Mel."

I place my hands on the table but do not take my eyes off of them. I push my chair back and stand straight up. "Are you talking to me?" They move back a little as I glare at them. "You men are lucky today. You got me in a good mood. I don't like people and I sure don't like them talking about my family. First of all, it's none of your goddamn business if I'm Mexican or white. But I'll tell you anyway because you asked. My dear ma is Mexican and I love her very much. My pa is German and I love him, too. Now if you two are making fun of my mother because she's Mexican, that's not too good because I will kill any man who says a bad word about her. Now if you're making fun of my pa, that'll get you killed, too, because nobody talks bad about my pa and lives to talk about it. If you're making fun of me because I am half Mexican and half white, that's not too good either because my ma and pa made me out of love."

"We didn't mean nothing. We're just talking, is all."

"See my knife?" I slam it onto the table. "It can go right through a man and come out the other side. It's killed a lot of men for less than what you are saying here to me today." They know I mean business. "Want some whiskey? It's Tennessee whiskey; the only kind I drink."

"Yeah," they nervously respond. "No hard feelings?"

"Have a seat."

They do so and chitchat about their pointless lives here in Texas. I don't say word. I just look at them as they talk.

Steve finally comments. "You don't talk much do you?"

"I don't talk much because I hate saying the same nonsense over and over again."

What I really want to point out is how much all these men need to bathe. They stink so bad and are all so dirty. Their hair and beards are the same way. Nothing has been washed around here in a long time. This whole place is quite filthy. But I'll just drink my whiskey and say nothing. Who knows, maybe tomorrow we die. But at least we got to drink this nice Tennessee whiskey first. If we get real lucky, maybe we'll get a pretty woman to sleep with before we leave this Earth.

A man walks in like he owns this cantina. Ha! It's William Travis!

Steve says, "What did we do wrong this time?"

Mel adds, "Whatever it is, he'll tell us. You can count on it."

Travis sees us. "Come sit with us, Mr. Travis!" says Steve.

He's all dressed up in a white coat and pants. He's the only one in here dress like that. His boots, though, are a light brown and his white hat has a single small feather in it.

"I want you meet a friend of ours, Mr. William Travis," Mel says.

"What's your name, young man?" Travis asks me.

"The name's Gunnar Best. You must be the William Travis I have heard so much about."

"Where you from, Mr. Best?"

"California. A little town you never hear of. It's so small, if you walk ten feet you're already in another town. That's how small it is."

As I speak, he looks at me like we're playing cards and he knows what I'm holding the whole time. His eyes never move.

"I hear you need men to fight at the Alamo," I comment. "I am ready to fight for Texas by your side, Mr. Travis."

"It's good to hear that. We could use another good man to fight."

"First, though, how much do you pay? I'd like to know before I put my life on the line."

150

"Nothing. You'd be a volunteer and get to fight the Mexican army for free. I figured you'd know that before coming all the way here."

"No, I thought I'd get paid good money killing Mexican men in this war. See, some people came through my town, El Sobrante, Mr. Travis—is it okay to call you Mr. Travis?" He nods. "They came in a wagon saying they needed men to fight at the Alamo. When someone needs someone, that usually means they will get paid for a job well done. It's for the money that I'm here, not for the fun of killing men."

"I see," he replies with a glare.

"I said to my brother, James, 'That sounds like some easy money. All I have to do is kill some Mexicans.' Don't get me wrong; I do like some Mexicans. My mother is Mexican and my father is German and they haven't killed each other the last time I saw them."

"A Mexican mother?" Travis asks.

"Yeah, I got Mexican blood in me. My brother wanted to come, too, but one of us had to stay home and take care of the place. I came to make the money we need to live. Wait until I tell my brother this. What is this world coming to? You kill someone and you don't even get paid. It reminds me of a time I asked this woman, 'How about a free one?' and she said I had to pay money if I wanted some honey."

"That's the way it is out here in Texas, Mr. Best, and I'm sorry you came all the way out here."

"How about a little money for the ladies? I still like honey. That should make up for something."

"Mr. Best, how about you take care of the woman out here and I'll take care of the Alamo. I can still use a man like you and your rifle, but I've got to go now. I'll see you men later. Don't drink too much. You're on duty all day tomorrow."

"Let me shake your hand, Mr. Travis, so I can tell my brother I shook the hand of the man in charge of the Alamo.

Shaking my hand he says, "At the Alamo, you will have place to eat and to sleep anytime you want, Mr. Best."

"Thank you, sir."

He walks to the door, stops and turns. "Remember, Mr. Best, we have a place for you there." Out the door he goes.

I get up from my chair and say, "I'll be right back."

I go to the bartender and ask, "What do you have to eat?"

"We got some good meat stew. It's got vegetables and comes with some bread, too."

"How much?"

"Dime."

"Sounds good." I drop my dime on the bar and he takes it.

He goes to the backroom and soon comes out with my meal.

Back at my table, I begin eating. "I know this food. I used to feed it to my pigs back home and they wouldn't eat it either."

Some men walk in. One of them looks familiar. I'm sure I've seen him in a picture. That's Davy Crockett standing there by the door in person. There are a dozen or so men with him, laughing at his jokes, and all wearing buckskin with their rifles by their sides.

I think I will walk over and try to talk to him. About what, I don't know, but I'll think of something. He watches me approach as I say, "You must be Davy Crockett from Tennessee."

"Do I know you?"

"My name is Gunnar Best. I'm from California. I came out here to Texas to fight at the Alamo."

"Every one of us is here for that reason, too, my friend. We like a good fight now and then, no matter it be against Mexicans or Creek Indians. And I think this time it's going to be a good fight. I got my good rifle with me, old Betsy, and these men from Tennessee will be fighting right beside me like we did with them Creek Indians."

"How would you like to sit with me at my table and have some Tennessee whiskey?" I suggest.

"I could go for that!"

Davy and some of his men come to my table. "I'll be right back, Davy." I get another bottle of whisky and a dozen glasses. "You men

152

don't have to tell me your names because I'll forget. But I am Gunnar Best and this is Steve and Mel."

They all exchange greetings.

I could see in Steve and Mel's eyes that they did not know who this man was. But I knew that this was Davy Crockett.

"I know you, Davy," I proclaim. "You were a congressman once."

"That's true. I was there in Washington D.C. But no more. Those damn voters didn't want me there anymore so I told 'em to go to hell. I said if you don't want my help in Washington D.C. then I'll go to Texas and help with their troubles instead."

One of his friends says, "Let's hear one of your jokes, Davy."

"Okay, here goes. This man was looking for a place to live but all the rooms were too expensive. So he asks this man, 'Do you have one I can afford?' He replies, 'Yes, it's only a dollar a month.' So the first man says, 'Let's see it!' So he shows him an outhouse and asks, 'How about it?' He says, 'I'll take it!' and gives the man the dollar for it. A month passes and he goes back to the landlord and says, 'I'm moving out!' 'Why?' he asks. 'Because the people downstairs are making too much noise and I can't get any sleep!'"

Everyone laughs but me.

"Where you from, Gunnar?" Davy asks.

"I live in California with my brother. We have some cattle and a few chickens there."

"You married?"

"We got a neighbor lady living with us. She lost her husband a while back. Indians got him. So we take care of her and she does our cooking, sewing and washing. But she's looking for a new husband. Her name's Debbie. She's pretty. Any man would love to have her. But I don't want her to get married because who's going to do all that work for us? We got a little creek through town and she's out there early in the morning scrubbing our clothes. She's got a nice rock out there, too—couldn't ask for anything better. And what does she want a husband for anyway? She's got me and my brother to take care of."

"Sounds like you have it all figured out," Davy responds.

"Davy, I want to ask you something. Do you think we'll win this war here at the Alamo?"

"Well, Gunnar, I do and I'll tell you why. Sam Houston asked me to come out here. He told me he was going to try and get some more men to help fight. He said he just needed a little more time. He has never lied to me and I think he will keep his word. With that, I think we'll have enough men to cover the Mexican Army. That's one of the reasons I came; to help my friend Sam. I have no doubt in my mind that we will win this battle here."

"But can you be so sure that Sam Houston will bring those men we need in time before the Mexican Army attacks?"

Davy looks at me and says, "Aren't you afraid of dying out here in Texas so far away from California? This isn't even your fight."

"No, Davy, and I'll tell you why. I've been in a lot of fights in my time with Indians and other men who wanted me dead. Some were good fights and others I figured some way to get out of it in time. I might fake that I'm dead, then get up and walk away. You know those Indians—sometimes there are too many and no way to win. But I still get out of it and live and fight another day. But if I have to die, I guess I will, but I will go out fighting to the end. I got my rifle here and it shoots good and that's all I care about—what I'm aiming at."

Davy says, "I know the odds are against us but I have faith in Sam Houston. He won't let us down. I'm willing to put my life on that."

"Well, men," I say, "I've got to get some sleep. So long, Davy."

"Bye, Gunnar. Hope you see you again."

As I leave the cantina and start down the street, Davy Crockett takes out his fiddle and begins to play. It's the dark of night out here now in San Antonio; a beautiful night. It's kind of lonely, though, for a man from the future walking down this street in 1836. I know that everyone in this town is dead a long time ago from my time. I get to the door of my hotel and look around this town before going in.

I open the door to my room and see my bag there. I look back to the manager and say, "Thank you, sir, for watching my bag for me."

"No problem, sir."

"Do you have any string?"

"Yes, I think so. Where, though, is the question... Here it is."

"Thanks."

I go to my room and take off my buckskin shirt and boots. I tie the string to my bag with the other end around my wrist. With my pistol and knife by my side, I try to get some sleep.

In the middle of the night, I feel my hand move. Looking around, I see a man by my bed trying to quietly pull my bag away.

I grab my pistol and shoot him in the face. Another man comes at me with a knife, so I grab mine and throw it, sticking him in the chest.

The hotel manager bursts in. "What happen here?"

"They tried to steal and now they're dead. I don't think I'll spend the night here again. I'll go to the Alamo where I know it's safe."

I get dressed, assemble my things and get out of there.

Walking down the road, I locate a horse stable. Searching around, I yell out, "Someone open the damn door, please!"

Finally, a man opens his window and looks down from the house. "Do you know how late it is? The stable is closed for the night!"

"I know that, but I need a horse anyways. I got money. Can you sell me a horse or not, big fellow?"

"Well, you already woke me up. I'll be down in a minute." With his hair a mess and wearing a dirty brown shirt and pants, he comes down and lets me in. "Which one do you like?"

I look at the horses one by one. "This one here. How much?"

"With a saddle, bridle and saddle blanket, it's going to cost you fifteen dollars."

"I got only united states silver dollars. Is that okay?"

"You bet! You might not believe me, and I don't care, but I think one day Texas will be part of the United States. Nobody believes me but that's what I think."

This man is big, but with no fat on him at all. Yet, he talks in a soft voice that I can barely hear.

"Sir, I believe you. I can see it in your face. Here is your money." I count out fifteen silver dollars for the man.

The man says, "Let me fix your horse for you."

He puts a saddle on and the bridle. I thank the man.

"Where are you going at this late hour?"

"I am going to the Alamo to fight the Mexican Army for Texas. What about you? Do you want to fight with us?"

"No, I'm too old. And I'm not stupid enough to die for nothing."

"What makes you say that?"

"Because William Travis doesn't know a thing about warfare. Just look around there. The grass is so tall, the Mexican Army could just walk right up to the front door and nobody could see them. And next door is a big building where Mexicans can shoot into the Alamo from. They should burn that thing down but they won't. Travis also don't have enough food for all his men or enough firewood."

"Well, let's hope for the best," I respond.

"Good luck, young man. I can tell you're not from around here. If you should get killed, I'll give you a good Catholic burial."

"Thanks. No one has ever said that to me before. I know we all think we'll outlive everyone else, but I'll live. What's your name?"

"Phil Coney."

"My name is Gunnar Best. I think God put you here on Earth for those who have no one else. Good-bye, my friend."

I hop onto my horse and ride toward the Alamo.

I think of Jack, who gave me my time machine. "Jack, thank you for the money you had in the trunk. It came in handy good. One day you and me will go out and raise hell somewhere in time. I miss you."

Chapter 14: **The Alamo**

I finally arrive at the Alamo! It actually isn't far from the stable.

And what Phil said was true. The grass is very tall.

The front door is locked but someone inside hears me trying to get in and shouts down from the window above. "Who goes there?"

"My name is Gunnar Best."

"What's your business?"

"William Travis told me to come if I want and so here I am."

"Wait there."

Eventually, I find Travis looking down from the window.

"Sir," I say, "is your offer still open for three meals and a place to sleep? If not, I shall go back to California where I belong."

"Let him in!" he shouts.

The front door opens and I go inside. It looks a lot different from the last time I saw it in the year 2000. In my time, it's a museum.

Travis approaches with Steve. "Good to see you, Gunnar," Travis says. He turns to Steve and orders, "Show our guest to the best room we have available."

"Yes, sir. I can tell by his buckskins he's a good fighter. They're good and old but have no holes from bullets or arrows. Look at mine. See all them holes. There's one here and one here. This one's the best. Indian shot me with an arrow. I still pulled it out and killed that damn Redskin who shot me."

This is the same man I was drinking with in the cantina. I almost killed him then. Now I'm glad I didn't.

"I'll catch up with you later, Mr. Best," says Travis as he departs.

Steve says, "Come with me, Gunnar. I'll show you the best room we got." I follow him up to a room with three beds. "This is it—your new home. How do you like it?"

"Cozy."

Today is my first day in Texas and in five days from now, the big fight will begin.

"Sleep well," says Steve as he gets ready for bed.

"Night, Steve."

I disrobe and take a look at my bed. It's made of rope. That's it. Just rope. You know, a hammock. This should be interesting.

My eyes crack open to the morning light. Turns out, I slept like a baby in that thing. Surrounding me are numerous other sleeping men.

A young man awakens and yells, "Get up men! We got to guard the gate from those Mexicans or they'll come in and kill us all."

Steve says to me, "Let's get something to eat first."

I notice the other man who was with us at the cantina, sleeping. Steve nudges him. "Time to get up, Mel."

"Five more minutes."

"Gunnar, put your clothes on and come with me."

I get dressed and look at my bed. That was definitely the best bed I ever slept on in my life.

I follow Steve to the kitchen. There's a big pot with some kind of stew in it. The cook slops it into bowls for us.

We sit at a table and eat. Wow, the food here is as dreadful as the food in the cantina. "You know what," I say, "I'll never make fun of my brother for his cooking again after this." It needs a little salt and pepper so I get some from my own stash.

"What you got there, Gunnar?"

"Salt and pepper gives it more flavor if you must know."

"Can I have some of your salt and pepper, please?"

"Yes, you may. Enjoy."

Before I know it, everyone is making use of my seasonings.

I eat my food this time because I'm hungry; not because it tastes good. I thought of what Phil said in the stable—that they don't have much here. This food with water will make a lot of food for the men. So I don't say a word about the meal.

"Steve, I'm going to the outhouse," I say.

I go to my room and get my bag.

I then go to the well, pull up a bucket of water and take it to the outhouse. Whew! It smells real bad. I look down the toilet and see all the shit the people of the Alamo have left. I plug it with my bucket so I don't have to look at it or smell it while I bathe. After all, there is no other way to take a bath here in Texas, so it's this or nothing.

I take my buckskins off. With a cup I use for coffee, I pour water over my head and face. I then wet my body and lather up some soap. After rinsing, I dry myself off and put my clothes back on.

Stepping outside, I find Steve standing there looking at me.

"What's up, Steve?"

"I came here to take a shit if you must know." He looks into my open bag. "What's that white roll of paper you got there?"

"Well, Steve, have you ever been to heaven?"

"Not yet. What kind of answer is that?"

"Well, Steve, after you take a shit, you use a newspaper to clean yourself, right? Using this instead feels like heaven."

"Can I use your roll of paper, then?"

"Yes, you can. I'll meet you later in our room."

"Okay, I will see you there when I'm done taking my shit."

In the next room, I find a seated man playing guitar, singing about some women he loves. A few others are present, thoroughly enjoying his music. He is good, too. Makes me think of women again out here where there are none. I do love women and I guess I always will.

Arriving back in my quarters, I find Mel lying in his bed.

I, too, lie down for a while until Steve bursts in and yells, "Hey, your toilet paper did feel just like heaven! You were right about that! It feels so good on my ass!"

"Glad to hear it."

"Where can I buy some of that toilet paper you got there?"

"You can't buy it here in Texas. Only in California. They passed a law not to sell toilet paper to people in other states."

"Can I buy this roll of toilet paper I used here?"

"No, but I'll give it to you. How about that?"

"You got a deal!

"Gunnar, after this war is over with, you and me and Mel should go out hunting. How does that sound to you?"

"Sounds good to me, Steve."

"This war ain't going to last long. Everybody knows that."

"What makes you so sure?"

"You see, Gunnar, you're from California so you don't know that we had this war before here in Texas. In 1835, this guy named Santa Anna heard of an armed resistance and sent his brother-in-law Martin Perfecto de Cos north with the Mexican army. Cos lost San Antonio and the Alamo on December 11th to us ragtag Texans led by Edward Burleson. It was a humiliating defeat and they went back to Mexico and promised never to come back here again. So this war is going to be a little one. You can count on it."

"I feel like something to drink. How about you, Steve?"

"Sure," he responds. "What about you, Mel?"

"I'll get up for a drink of Tennessee whisky any day."

We go to our horses and saddle up. Passing through the gates of the Alamo, we make our way to the cantina. Walking in, I say to the bartender, "A bottle of Tennessee whisky and three glasses, sir."

"That'll be three dollars."

"No problem. Here you go."

I go to a table where my friends await. They see my bottle and are drawn to it like flies because I know they have no money.

I notice a pretty girl just standing there. She wears a long, brown dress with red lines. You can't see her legs; just her shoes. I walk up to her ask, "Would you like to dance?"

"Why, yes."

Maybe I'll get lucky tonight. I get close and put my arm around her. She smells quite bad. Like my friends, it looks like she has not seen a bar of soap for some time now.

"She tells me, "You smell so good. I could eat you up, mister, the way you smell."

I look to Mel and say, "Mel, come over and dance with this pretty young woman and have a good time."

She gives me a puzzled look.

Mel quickly arrives and takes over for me. He seems quite happy to have a woman in his arms. After all, there are no women to dance with at the Alamo. They're all either married, too old or too young.

A man walks in and sees her dancing with Mel. He storms over and throws Mel down to the floor. I get up from my chair, walk over to him and look him in the eye. "You just pushed my friend here to the floor and I haven't heard an apology from you yet, sir."

"And you're not about to," the man says.

"Well, that's okay with me but what about old Sally here?" I point to my bowie knife. "If you are not going to say you're sorry to her, she'll make a dead man out of you."

"I don't know no Sally."

"Well, I will fix that for you. I pull my bowie knife and say to her, "This bad man here pushed our friend. What do you think we should do about this?" I put the blade to my ear. "My knife says to kill you if you don't say you're sorry." He looks at me, confused. "Between you and me, my knife likes to kill people. What's that?" I place the knife against my ear once more. "My knife says to count to ten and if you don't say you're sorry, you are a dead man."

Confused, the man finally arrives at a decision. "Yes, I'm going to say I'm sorry to your friend here."

"That's good to know." I turn my back to him and walk away.

He lifts his flintlock rifle and shoots me in the back but the bullet just impacts my spine and falls to the floor.

I slowly turn. Glaring, I walk to the man and say, "Did you know that today will be your last day alive in this cantina? So long, friend." I pull old Sally and send her right through the man. Now he is dead; all for the love for a woman that stinks. What a stupid man.

Steve gets up and asks, "Why didn't that bullet kill you?"

"That fool must not have wrapped his bullet in cloth and it just rolled down the barrel when he fired."

"Yeah—"

"Let's go, Steve. Killing takes all the fun out of being here."

We step outside and head down the street.

Steve says, "First time I killed a man, I could not sleep for weeks. I was in El Paso, drinking in a cantina. This man was making fun of me because of the way I look. He was a well-dressed city man and got a lot of other people laughing at me, too. They did not know I could hear what he was saying. At first, I did not say a word. I just sat there looking at him. Then, he pointed at me. That did it. I picked up my rifle and I aimed it at his big mouth. He knew he was going to die and I know he heard the sound of my rifle fire before he died. Everyone looked at me but no one was laughing then. I went out to my horse but this man's face kept coming back to me. It don't go away neither. I know how you feel, Gunnar."

"Let's get back to the Alamo," I suggest as we hop on our hoses.

On the way back, I see cows. "Let's go to that house up ahead." I see a man who looks the owner and ask, "I want to buy some cows. How much do you want for them?"

"Ten dollars a head."

"I'll take twenty, then. Here's two hundred in gold." I count it out.

"No problem," the stunned man responds.

Arriving at the Alamo, they see us returning with the cows and let us in. We put the animals away and I look for the cook and tell him, "Cook me up a nice steak, will ya?"

Travis approaches. "How did you get all them cows?"

"Gold, Mr. Travis."

"Thank you, Mr. Best. How did you know we were low on food?"

"I just got tired of the food you had. No steak? This is Texas, man, not California! What's wrong with you here? So I bought some."

The cook barbeques one cow and I get my steak. And it is good.

After dinner, Travis gets up and says, "Mel, Steve and Gunner—go to the front gate and take watch tonight."

As I rise, I look around and see that everyone is quite happy after their meal.

At the front gate, we huddle around a fire while standing guard. Under the Texas stars, we talk about women and life until a familiar-looking man rolls a barrel of gunpowder over and sits.

"Hello there," he says to me. "My name is Jim Bowie."

I am flustered for a moment. "I'm Gunnar Best from California."

"Yes, Travis told me about you. You thought you were going to get paid out here but found no money. Yet, you stayed anyway and bought those cows for us to eat. That was nice of you, Gunnar."

"My father always said when we were growing up that there are three things in life that you must have to live good: that you eat well, have nice clothes and a good place to live. If you fail on one of those, you're not living the good life that God wanted you to have. I was not eating good here so I got the cows."

"Your father sounds like a wise man. One day, I will tell my boy that same thing." He looks to Steve. "Why are you at the Alamo ready to fight the Mexicans when you might die out here?"

"Well, Mr. Bowie, I have land here in Texas and I'm not going let them damn Mexicans come over and take it away from me and my family without a fight."

"And you, Mel?"

"I built a home here in Texas. Everything I got is here. If I lose it, I lose everything I worked for and will have nothing. A man's gotta fight for his home and his woman. I don't have no children yet but hope to in time."

"What about you, sir?" I ask Bowie.

"I've obtained about seven hundred and fifty thousand acres of land out here in Texas. I am not going to let anyone tell me to get the hell off it. I have a wife, children and slaves to think about."

"You have slaves?"

"Oh, sure. That's a lot of land to take care of."

"What about you, Gunnar? Do you have slaves where you live?"

"No, it's against the law there."

"I'm sorry to hear that. The black man can help you on your land and make you a lot of money. It's a good deal. You buy him and use him for two to five years and then sell him for what you paid and get a better one down the road."

"But I hear the blacks suffer at the hand of the white man."

"You see, a black man is like a child. When he does something wrong, he must pay for it. But I'll say this—they got it easy with me. They start when the sun comes up and go home went it goes down. They love me for that. I'm a good man to them. You can ask anyone."

I am not sure how to respond.

"Gunnar, can I see your knife there?" Reluctantly, I hand it to him and he inspects it. "Bigger than mine! Nice."

"Thank you, Mr. Bowie."

"You don't have to call me "mister," son. I am not William Travis after all. He was a schoolteacher and attorney at one time and so it went to his head. Mister this and mister that."

"Okay, Jim."

"How do you like your knife?"

"I love it, but people on the other end of it don't like it so much if you know what I mean. I found that if I throw it, the tip of the blade must be pointing down or it won't stick in the wall or person."

"I do know what you're talking about. I'm afraid I've killed more than I can count."

He looks up to the beautiful stars with sadness in his eyes. "Have you ever gambled for love and lost?"

"I think we all have at some point."

"I don't think you get what I mean. One time down in Louisiana, I went with this lovely young lady for a drink and I saw a card game. If you know me, you know I love to play cards. We walked over and I asked if I could join in. A fat man with a big cigar in his mouth said,

'If you got money. If you don't, get the hell out.' Grinning, I took a chair beside him. As he dealt, I could see him staring at my woman. I understand. So no big deal. I told her this would not last long. After a while, a large pile of money accumulated on the table. The fat man then bet more money than I had. My hand was good—two kings and queens—and I figured he had nothing. So I said, 'Sir, can I write you an I.O.U.?' He told me, 'No money, no game. We told you that when you sat down.' 'What about my knife?' 'No.' 'Then tell me what you want!' He locked eyes with my lady. I got up and she said to me. 'Let me see your hand first.' I showed her my cards. She looked at the pot and said, "I get half.' I nodded. 'I call you now,' I told him. The man laid down his cards. Full house. He looked to her and said, 'Guess you belong to me now.' She looked to me, pleadingly. 'He won, fair and square, my love. 'Nice game,' he said, 'but I'm going to bed early tonight.' She said, 'Sir, I want you to know I'm a lady.' 'Maybe now, but you won't be tonight.' As he took her away, she looked to me for help. But she was gone and I never saw her again. So, Gunnar, ever gamble for love and lose?"

"No, not like that. But if it were me playing that game, if I had your hand and no more money, I would have just stopped and went home with that young lady by my side."

Somberly, he says, "It's almost daytime. Would you three mind going out and looking for that Mexican Army for me?"

"Yes, sir." Steve replies.

As we saddle up, William Travis comes out and asks Jim, "Where are those men going?"

"I told them to go on out and look for the Mexican Army."

"You had no right to do that!"

"Let's just get one thing straight, Mr. Travis. James C. Neill and I were here first. All the men here do what I say and you know it. Besides, I'm fourteen years older so I know a lot more than you."

"You're damn lucky we're on the same side of this war, Bowie! But you remind me of an old dog. And every dog has its day."

"You name the time and place and I'll be there! Good day, sir."

Witnessing this, none of us or the other men present utter a word as Bowie storms away from Travis.

As me, Steve and Mel leave the comforts of the Alamo, the doors shut behind us. We are on our own now.

Chapter 15: **The Mexican Army**

Up ahead, I can see the cantina with a man and woman going in. It's kind of early for drinking, so we just ride on.

There's nothing out here but grass, weeds and rock.

A bit farther down the road, I can see the ranch where we bought the cattle. But no one is around. Just cattle.

Continuing on, we ride along a road next to the San Antonio River and see what lay beyond.

Hearing a noise on the other side, we locate a safe place to cross. Reaching a hill, we leave our horses at the bottom and climb up the steep slope. Cautiously, we peer over the tip of the hill.

Holly Moses! Talk about an army! There are thousands of soldiers spread across the land in thousands of tents with thousands of rifles, cannons—everything! I've never seen anything like this.

One of them sits on a white horse while hitting another man with a small whip and laughing. I don't know what he did to deserve that but it doesn't settle well with me.

I look over to Steve and can tell he feels the same.

I take my rifle and pour power into the barrel. I wrap a bullet in a cloth and drive it down with a rod. After sprinkling a small amount of power near the flint, I take careful aim at the Mexican upon his horse. Slowly, I squeeze the trigger. My shot blazes through his throat. He grabs his neck with both hands and falls to the ground.

With all hell breaking loose, I suggest to Steve, "Let's get the hell out of here before we all get killed."

We run down the hill, hop on our horses and ride like crazy.

Shots begin whizzing past our ears as countless Mexican soldiers take chase. Mel's horse is shot and he goes down. I charge back for my friend and yell, "Give me your hand!" I pull him up onto my horse and we race all the way back home.

They see us coming and swing open the gates long enough for us to enter. Safely inside, Bowie runs up as we get off our horses.

"What happened?" he asks.

I'm just about to answer when William Travis runs up and shouts, "What did you see out there?"

I look to Bowie and respond, "There were—"

"Report to me!" Travis shouts.

"I'm reporting to the man or sent me on my mission, sir."

"But I'm in charge here, not him!"

"The way I hear it, you both are." Travis glares at me and Bowie. Sensing the tension I say, "Sorry, Mr. Travis. I know you're in charge as well. My mom always said I was very hard headed. But there's no time for this. There are thousands of Mexican soldiers close by and they are heavily armed. There's no way out of it."

"Thank you, men," Bowie tells us three, "for putting your lives on the line for the rest of us. I owe you one."

"You don't owe us nothing. Just doing our job."

Worried, Travis walks away.

I walk to where my horse is tied and remove his saddle, blanket and bridle before feeding and watering him.

Nearby, I notice two Mexicans talking in Spanish. One is shorter than the other. I approach. "Hey, there. My name is Gunnar Best."

The taller one asks, "Are you Mexican or white?"

"Well, if you must know, my mother was from Mexico and my father from Germany."

"Do you speak Spanish?" the shorter one asks.

"Just a little."

"We speak just a little English."

They both wear big sombreros on their heads.

"So you men are fighting for Texas and not Mexico. Why?"

"In Mexico, the rich get richer and the poor get poorer. Not here. A man can make a living here in Texas. I have a home and family. Mexico wants to come and take it away but they can go to hell. They have to kill me first. They know me in Mexico. They know I will not take any shit from them."

"Me, too," the other Mexican says. "But what about you, Gunnar? Why are you out here fighting for Texas?"

"I'll tell you the truth. At first, it was for the money but now it's for Texas and the people who live here and who will die here for it."

"When this war is over, I hope you'll come and meet my family. My home is your home; anytime you come to Texas. And my wife is a good cook. I know you will like it. See you later."

"Adios," I respond.

I head to the kitchen where the cook notices me and asks, "What do you want here, Mr. Best?"

"Well, I'm hungry."

He cuts me a slab of meat and cooks it with beans, rice and bread. Nice change from the slop I got when I first arrived.

Steve and Mel enter and sit with me.

Mel asks, "So what does your house look like in California?"

"It's kind of modern."

"What do you mean by 'modern'?" Steve asks.

"Well, we got water in the house."

"Water?" Mel asks. "In the house? How?"

"It's pretty easy. My brother thought of it when we got the land. Me and him dug a well and then built the house over it. If we need water, we just pull the bucket up and don't have to go outside. The only problem is our floors are all dirt until we can get some money for wood. Until then, you can say our floors are always dirty."

The dining hall door swings open. Jim Bowie walks in and sits at one of the tables and look at me. He takes his knife out of its holster and sets it on the table. He plays with it for a bit before getting up and walking over. "Gunnar, you really any good with that knife of yours?"

"There's no one better than me with a knife. That, I know."

"Why don't we just find out how good you are, then?"

"Well, Jim, I like you and you know that. I don't want to hurt your feelings when you find out I'm little bit better than you with old Sally here by my side. But I'm game."

He says to Steve, "Go ahead and lean that table against the wall." With the table in place, Bowie takes his knife and gouges an X on it. He takes ten steps back and throws his blade, striking the X dead center. He yanks it from the wood. Raising an eyebrow, he smirks at me. "Now let's see what you can do with that thing you call a knife."

I go to where he stood and pull my knife. I stare at the mark on the table and hurl my blade. To everyone's surprise, it misses the table entirely and sticks into the wall. I retrieve old Sally when Jim asks, "What the hell happened?"

I show him the tip of my knife. "Oh, I saw a bug. I hate bugs, so I killed it." Clearly, half of a fly is smeared against the shiny metal.

As the men squint, I startle them by throwing my knife at the X and it goes right through the table.

Stunned, Jim says, "Damn. That knife of yours is something else!"

I respond, "I don't like to play around with it. But when I stick somebody with it, I like them to stay against the wall for while."

Jim shouts, "Ha! You're damn good, sir! No question about it. If anybody says anything, you tell them I said you're as good with that knife as me. I just wanted to see with my two eyes if you were really any good or if you're just talk."

"Well I'm glad we settled that."

The men put the table back and we leave the dining hall. Bowie heads toward the stables and I head back to my room.

Lying in my bed, I hear a knock out in the hallway. Quietly, I step to my door and place my ear against it.

A door opens and a young lady asks, "Is Jim here?"

A black man replies, "No, Ms. Alyssa. But he'll be back soon."

"Can I come in and wait?"

"Yes, but I don't know when he'll—"

"It doesn't matter. It's you I want to see anyway." I hear her step inside and shut the door. I move to the wall and put my ear against it. "You know," she continues, "you're just a slave and not a real person. You know you're not even a real man, don't you? Speak up!"

170

"Yes, I know that, Ms. Alyssa."

"You know if I whip you, you can do nothing about it don't you?"

He doesn't respond.

"Do you want me to whip you now?"

"No, Ms. Alyssa."

"Well, then, you must do what I tell you."

"Whatever you want."

"Take your clothes off."

"Ms. Alyssa?"

"Do as you're told!"

It sounds like he's doing it.

Through this thin wall, I hear her walking across the room. "You know, where I live, we have many slaves and they all do what I tell them or they know I'll beat them." As she speaks, I believe I can hear her taking off her clothes, too. "Do I look pretty to you? Would you like to touch my beautiful white body with your black hands?" I hear her unsnapping something on her dress.

"Miss..."

"Yes, I'd like your big lips on my big breasts..."

I hear their door open. Bowies shouts, "What the hell's going on?"

Alyssa responds, "Mr. Bowie! I came to see you but you weren't here. Enu told me to come on in and wait. So I did and he told me he likes white women and he was looking at my body..."

"That's not true!" Enu blurts out. "You know me, Mr. Bowie. You know I wouldn't do that."

Alyssa shouts, "Mr. Bowie! You're a man and you know a man will lie to be with a woman. This black pig wanted a white woman and he would've done anything to have me. We're not safe around his kind! He said if I didn't, he was going to kill me. I was afraid and felt I better do what he told me. Now I feel dirty all over."

Bowie looks to Enu and frowns.

"I never touched her, sir!" Enu says.

"Sir," she says, "I have never been with any man until this black animal raped me. I was helpless to stop him. He was the first to ever lay hands on my beautiful white skin and now I have the nightmare of knowing my first man was a black slave. I won't ever be able to give myself to a white man after this because now he will ever want me for a wife or as the mother of his babies."

Bowie gives her a skeptical look.

"I need to know that you believe me, a white woman, and not this lying slave!"

"Just calm down, Alyssa."

"I want you to kill him right now for what he did to me! What white woman in her right mind would want a black man anyway?"

"Okay," Mr. Bowie replies, "I believe you and I promise no one will ever know what happened here." He looks to Enu. "You are not to tell anyone about this or I will have you skinned alive."

"I won't, sir."

Bowie turns to Alyssa. "I know he won't tell anyone and I won't either. Just make sure you keep your mouth shut, too."

Alyssa hugs Bowie and begins to sob.

Bowie tells her, "I think this is my fault. Once a year I give Enu a slave woman to be with. Maybe it was not enough.

"Enu," he orders, "outside!" He then picks up a rope.

"Mr. Bowie! She's lying! You must believe me. I would never—"

Jim pays no attention and shoves him out.

I step out of my room to find Bowie shoving Enu through the hall. I follow them outside.

Bowie shouts, "You two men take off his shirt and tie this slave against that pole."

Travis rushes forward. "What's going here?"

Jim replies, "He's my slave, my property to do with as I wish."

Travis knows he can say nothing.

Bowie starts whipping the black man.

172

As the whip comes down again and again, Enu yells, "I didn't do anything wrong! Mr. Jim, please believe me!"

Knowing what happened, I can't stand by and do nothing. "Stop!"

"Stay out of this. Ain't none of your business. I have to keep these slaves in line. I'm going to whip his black ass until he's unconscious and then I'm going to gut him like I do one of my hogs. If you had slaves of your own you'd understand."

This is wrong but I'm helpless to do anything about it. In my time, to do this to another man is against the law but this is 1836. I watch him being beaten by my friend and I feel so bad for him.

Bowie appears weakened and finally stops. "Enu, I'm setting you free." Shocked, all the onlookers gasp. "I do this because I feel I will die soon when those damn Mexicans come. Go. I never want to see your black face in this part of the country again."

Through his pain, Enu shows relief.

As Enu staggers off, Jim walk over to a man, takes his musket and shoots Enu in the back. Enu drops dead and Bowie walks away.

Alyssa runs to Jim and asks, "Why did you kill him?"

He answers in a quiet voice, "Because he had a taste of a white woman and I knew he would want to be with another. So I felt I had to put an end to it and set an example for my other slaves.

Like an animal, he killed a person without thinking twice about it.

But I know that black men will never stop wanting white women, because white women will never stop wanting them.

I go to the mess hall for some chow. The soldiers there eat their food and I don't say a word to Bowie because of what he did.

A young woman wipes down tables. When I look to her, she looks quickly away. Bowie notes this, too.

Travis walks in and looks around. "I need a volunteer to go look for Sam Houston. We might not make it if he doesn't come help us."

I stand and say, "I'll cross that Mexican line and go look for him."

Steve stands and says, "No, Gunnar. I'll go. I'm faster."

"I'm more than able, I assure you."

"But you're from California and I'm from Texas. You don't know your way around these parts like I do and that would make you an easy target for the Mexicans."

Travis says to Steve, "If you can deliver this message to Houston, you won't have to come back and fight with us. We'll understand."

"We'll see about that, Mr. Travis."

I say to Steve, "You probably are better equipped than me. Just take care of yourself and I'll see you when and if you return."

Travis adds, "When you leave the Alamo, walk your horse as long as you can, so he won't get tired on you. You might need him if the Mexican Army discovers you're going for help. When the enemy line is behind you, ride him as fast as you can."

"Understood, sir." He looks to all the men, as if for the last time. "I will leave now and do my job for Texas."

I catch up to him in the hall and look him in the eye. "When this war is over," I tell him, "you and I are going hunting. Mel, too. You take care of yourself and don't let one of those Mexican soldiers shoot you in the ass. And say 'hello' to Sam Houston from Gunnar Best."

"I'll do that for you, my friend. You got my word, Gunnar."

I watch Steve walk out to the stable and prepare his horse. He then heads through the gates of the Alamo. He rides away and I can hear gunshots in the distance. After that, I see or hear nothing.

I head back to my room very slowly, thinking of Steve and those gunshots. I hope he made it out okay.

My thoughts then turn to Debbie and my brother, James, talking about the Alamo and how I thought it would be fun to go here and be with Davy Crockett and Jim Bowie; like it was some kind of game or vacation. Boy, was I wrong. I realize now how serious this situation is and the fact that people's lives are on the line. Worst of all, I know the end of the story. I know that everyone here will die and that's a fact. The other thing is, I know I can leave here any time I want to, so my life will be spared. I like Steve, Mel, Bowie, Davy Crockett and even William Travis. But I know all of these men will die soon and there is nothing I could or should do about it. I will go back home like nothing happened but these men will live in my heart until the day I die.

Mel comes in and sits. "We're totally outnumbered here, Gunnar. I know we will die soon along with everyone else." He seems to know his fate. "I have a home, but I don't have a wife or children and now I never will. I'm only twenty-five and my world will stop here. It's just not right for me to die this way, but I know this is the end."

"Yeah, I get it."

"I don't know how close you were with your father, Gunnar, but I was very close to mine. He told me to keep our family name alive as long as I can. So you see, if I die here in the Alamo, my family name will die with me. I can't let that happen, but I have no way to stop it."

"You're right. All the men will die here. The odds are definitely against us and I think everyone here knows that. I don't think anyone expects help to arrive in time. But if you decide not to fight, I will not respect you any less. I think you are a brave man just for being here and to do what you came here to do."

Mel sighs.

"You know, I am half Mexican and I know the Mexican people. They will let the women and children go before the fight begins. You can go with them and not die here. But that's a decision you, and you alone, will have to make."

"I guess I owe it to my father and our family name. But let's just go to sleep and see what happens tomorrow."

"Good night, then."

Chapter 16: **The Tension Builds**

The next morning we get up and go to breakfast. As I pile food onto my plate, I hear an explosion outside.

We all rush out and I see part of the outer wall collapsed. I climb up the wall and see Davy Crockett doing the same.

Davey shouts, "We need to take out those men shooting all them cannons if we're going to stand a chance!"

I know my gun is old, and I'm not sure if I can hit those men from this far away, but I have to do something or this fight will be over before it begins. If I get into my time machine and become invisible, it'd be easy. But I must be careful not to change the course of history. I know many men will die here today and I must force myself to not change anything that is going to happen.

Davey says to us, "Looks like they're just trying to weaken our defenses for an attack later. Men, the time is near."

We spend the day patching the wall as best we can. It's dark now and I station myself on one of the walls and take watch. I don't see anyone, but I notice the sky and its many stars. It's so beautiful. I only wish I had a beautiful woman to look at them with me.

Sitting on a barrel of gun powder, I think of the times I would go to the mall and have a cup of coffee and look at all of the beautiful women. Sometimes I'd even ask them to sit and have a cup with me.

Now I sit here with my gun, Ole Betsy, by my side, surrounded by the walls of the Alamo.

I know a lot of women out there, and I know they think they know me, but they don't because I'm a time traveler and they would never have guessed that.

Here I am on the wall of the Alamo practically talking to myself. Boy have I lost it. I guess I have never been all alone like this before. Just me and my gun and the sky with all the beautiful stars up there.

I hear a noise behind me. "Who's there?" I ask.

"It's Jim Bowie, Gunnar. Don't shoot."

"I won't, Mr. Bowie. What are you doing out here?"

"Travis told me where you were, so I came to see how you were doing and if you needed someone to talk to." He sits. "You know, some people say this is the end of the line for us all."

"Could be."

"I was thinking, when you die, some people will say you were a good man. Others will say you were no good. We will die, and I know that. Some will undoubtedly say bad things about me. But if one of us survives, he could tell them the truth. Should you die, Gunnar, I won't let anybody talk bad about you. If I die—"

"Say no more. You are my friend and nobody better say anything bad about you. But if you should die here at the Alamo, it will hurt, because you are not just a friend but a blood brother to me."

He says, "You know, I wish I would have known you a long time ago. We could have been the best of friends. Now, only death awaits us and there is nothing we can do."

I look up at the stars.

"You know, I think Becka likes you," he tells me. "I saw it in her eyes today; the way she looks at you."

"Becka?"

"She cleans up in the mess hall. You saw her there today."

"Oh, right."

Bowie looks me in the eye with a smirk on his face. Confused, I just frown at him. He subtly nods in a direction behind us. From there, I hear a faint thud and ask, "Do you hear something?"

"I don't hear anything at all."

I hear it again and pick up my rifle.

"It's me, Becka. Don't shoot."

I give Bowie a look and he grins.

"What are you doing out here this late?" I ask.

"Don't worry, my father won't find out I'm here. I saw Mr. Bowie and asked if I could come up here with you."

"Well, keep your head down."

She climbs up. "You can see a long way from here."

There is a single gunshot in the distance and Becka yelps. There is another shot and Becka collapses and falls fifteen feet to the ground. Bowie and I rush down to her.

I hold her in my arms and touch her hair, softy. Looking into her eyes, I can see that she is in a lot of pain.

She whispers, "Gunnar, I don't want to die," as she grabs hold of my buckskin shirt.

"You'll live. You have my word."

Bowie looks upon Becka there on the ground and says, "Gunnar, you better start a fire. I'll take that bullet out myself."

"Shouldn't we take her to a doctor?"

"Yes, but where in the hell is a doctor way out here? Unless you want to ask the Mexican Army."

William Travis charges over to us. "I heard shots from my office. What the hell is going on? How did she get shot on your watch?"

I reply, "She wanted to come up, so I let her."

"Gunnar, what's so hard about watching this wall? Do I have to tell you everything? You should know not to bring a woman up there! This is your fault and if she dies, that will be your fault, too."

He abruptly storms away.

"Bowie, what are we going to do for her?"

"Like I told you, I'll take the bullets out. Just start that damn fire so I can see what I'm doing."

I dash to some wood I see by the stables and pull some dry grass. When I return, I quickly get the fire started.

Bowie says, "Lift up her dress and see if she has anything white on and then cut it off. We'll need it to stop the bleeding when we take the bullet out."

"Why just the white material?"

"The colors on the dress have dye in them. I have a stone in my bag to sharpen my knife with. I better do that before I operate."

After he does so, he moves his blade over the fire to sterilize it.

Finally, Jim says, "Becka, this is going to hurt. I am sorry I don't have anything to ease your pain, but I'm going to do the best I can to save your life and that's what's important. I want you to put this piece of wood in your mouth and bite down hard. It will help you tolerate the pain. Don't stop until I tell you."

Becka asks, "Will I die here? Is today my last? Tell me the truth."

"No, Becka. Everything will be okay. Don't worry."

"Have you ever done this before?" I ask.

"Many times. It's good to know how to do these things. Out here, there are no doctors when you need them. Now let's get started."

Becka moans as she bites hard on the piece of wood. I can tell she is in serious pain. Finally, Bowie locates the bullets and gently takes them out. There's a lot of blood, so he uses the white material to soak it up and apply pressure. Next, he takes thread and sews the wounds.

"Let's put her in that wagon there and cover her with a blanket," he tells me. We lay her there and he says, "I'm beat. That took all the energy I had. I think she's going to be okay, but the next twenty-four hours will be critical. She was pretty lucky. One of the bullets went straight through her and the other wasn't in too deep."

Becka continues to moan in pain but there's no medication we can give her. I feel so bad for her, but there's nothing I can do.

A few men struggle to position a cannon on the other side of the compound where the wall was blown apart earlier.

"Keep her covered up, Gunnar. I'll be right back. I'm going to see what those men are trying to do with that cannon."

I notice another man walking toward me. He does not look happy. I say "hello" but his response is a punch in the face. As I get up, my eyes are on him and I pull my knife. I will kill this man for hitting me.

Becka shouts, "Father, don't hurt him! He saved my life!"

I put my knife back in its sheath.

"Becka, you okay?"

"Yes, Father. Gunnar and Jim Bowie saved me."

"William Travis said it was Gunnar's fault that you got shot."

180

"That's not true. It was my fault. Gunnar told me to stay down but I didn't listen."

"Why the hell did you come out here in the first place at this time of night? Don't you know it's dangerous out here?"

"Because I like Gunnar. He's a good man and I'm sure he would not let anything happen to me. This was an accident and was entirely my fault, so don't blame him."

All I can do is watch. I don't know if I should say anything or not so I decide to keep my mouth shut.

"Father, you're right. Please take me home now. Mother must be worried to death."

I tell her, "I am so sorry, Becka. I never wanted anything bad to happen to you. Get on home. It's too dangerous here."

"I'll get a cart," her father says.

I feel bad about what happened, but she is young and will recover thanks to Mr. Bowie.

I go where Jim went to help out with the cannon. He's standing on a ladder, trying to push it on top of the wall but the ladder breaks. Jim falls and the cannon crashes onto his chest.

"Get that off him! Hurry!" I shout.

They heave the ladder off but I can see that he's in a lot of pain.

Damn it. I bought all the things I thought I'd need but didn't think to get any medical supplies that could help my friends now.

"One of you go to that wagon and get a blanket." I kneel down to Jim. I think he has some broken ribs.

We place the blanket over him and take him to his room.

William Travis comes in. Jim, coughing, explains what happened, but in a rude way.

Mr. Travis says nothing and leaves.

"Jim," I ask, "why did you talk so harshly to Mr. Travis?"

He replies, "When you're down, never talk about it to people who do not like you."

"I'll let you rest."

As I depart Jim's room, I hear someone yell, "Open the gate!"

I rush outside to see what's going on.

It's Steve riding in!

I run up and wrap my arms around him. "It's so good to see you again, my friend. I didn't know if you were alive or dead!"

"It's been interesting."

"Did you find Sam Houston?"

"Yes, I did."

"What did he say?"

But before Steve could answer me, Travis storms over and says, "This information is for me only. Come, Steve. Let's talk in my office without any interruptions."

With nothing else to do, I go to my room and sleep.

The next morning I find Steve and Mel near the front gate.

"So what happened out there with Sam Houston?" I ask.

"Nothing. He says he doesn't have the men to send us."

"Then why did you come back?"

"Travis said we need help or everyone here will die. I could either come back and fight or run away and hide. I believe in the freedom I am fighting for. I'm no quitter. I said that before. I will stay here and fight the Mexicans for my land, my home and my country. I won't let any man tell me to get out. I think every man here feels the same."

Looking at his proud face, I feel shame because I already know that all of these men will die soon by the hands of the Mexican Army. Yet, I will continue to live because I have my time machine and can go back home where I belong. I want to tell them what will happen, but I can't change history. I have to let it happen as it was meant to.

Jack never told me that sometimes being a time traveler will hurt. Now I know what being a time traveler means. Things happen beyond our control that we are helpless to change. We can alter the future but we can't never really change the past no matter how bad we want to.

Steve says, "Why so sad? Something I said?"

I know I can't tell him the truth. "I was just thinking about all of us getting killed and that time is running out. I just wish there was something we could do to stop this so no one would have to die. I think of all of you as my family."

Steve leans in close and says, "I need another one of those white toilet paper rolls you gave me."

"What happen to the one I gave you?"

"Well, you're not going to believe this, but when I was away, I went to take a shit and when I came out, there was Sam Houston, waiting. He asked me what was that roll of paper was in my hand. I told him, 'Have you ever been in heaven?' He said, 'No. What kind of answer is that?' I said, 'If you use this roll of paper on your ass, then you will know, Mr. Houston.' So I gave him my roll of toilet paper. Later that day, he said, 'It's true. I did feel like I was in heaven.' He also said, 'Steve, I know you're good man, but if you go back to the Alamo you will die fighting there. If you stay here, you will live. It's better to live and fight another day.' I told him, 'Mr. Houston, I will go back and be with my friends and I will die there with my friends.'"

A man on the wall yells, "A rider is coming! He has a white flag!"

"Hold your fire!" Travis shouts. "Let's see what he wants."

Stopping outside of the gate, the rider yells with a heavy Spanish accent, "Any of you that want to live can put your guns down and walk out. We will let you go as well as the women and children. This is the only chance you will get. If you stay, all of you will die."

I climb a ladder and look into the distance. I see a Mexican Army officer looking at Travis and Travis staring him straight in the eye.

Again, the messenger warns, "If you don't lay down your arms and leave now, all of you here will die for nothing. This place is not worth dying for!"

I run to find Jim Bowie.

I find him in his room as two young soldiers tell him, "There is a Mexican Army soldier outside the gate talking to William Travis."

"I need you men to help me to the gate immediately."

As Bowie arrives at the main gate, the Mexican soldier rides off. Travis comes down from the wall.

Bowie asks, "What did they say?"

"They want us to lay down our arms. They say we can leave with the women and children or be killed."

"What can we expect from Sam Houston?"

"Nothing."

The men all look at each other with unease.

Travis shouts, "If any of you choose to put your guns down and walk away, no one will think any less of you." He draws a line in the dirt. "Whoever's with me, stand on this side of the line. Those who wish to leave, stand on the other."

All of the men except one stand on the side with William Travis. Even Jim Bowie, in much pain, gets up. Only Mel chooses to leave.

Travis says to him, "Get all the women and children together."

I walk to Mel and give him a hug because I know he needs one. "Just remember one thing. You'll always be my friend no matter what happens here."

He responds, "I want you to have my rifle so you can kill some of those Mexicans for me." He then looks to the others with a sad face and walks away.

Soon, all the women and children are ready to leave and all their wagons are packed up.

I see Becka, so beautiful, lying in a wagon. I go over and tell her, "Have a good life. Enjoy it. I hope you'll always remember us all who fought here at the Alamo for our country."

Overcome with grief, she takes my hand but is unable to respond.

In the next wagon, I see one of the cleaning women, Raquel, with her husband. He puts something in her hand. They don't know I'm watching as he gives her a kiss and walks away, probably thinking that this is the last time he will ever see her. I wave goodbye. It was really nice knowing her.

The wagons move out and the gates to the Alamo slowly close. I climb up the ladder and watch them go over the little hill.

It hurts to look at these men and know they will die at the start of their lives. All for a piece of Texas.

Davy Crockett walks over. "You know, Gunnar, I've been in a lot of fights in my time, and in many of those, the odds were against me. But somehow, I was always able to get out of it. This time, though, I don't think so. I knew this day would come, but I never thought it would all end here at the Alamo. I am not afraid to die. And if I must, I will die for the freedom of my country. How about you?"

"I was always sure I'd die jumping from some woman's window with her husband gunning me in the back. My weakness is women. I just can't help myself."

Travis comes out and shouts, "Each of you men grab three rifles out of the wagon! Many of you will die her today, but the cause you fight for is great and you will always be remembered for this fight at the Alamo. God be with us all. Let's show those Mexicans what we're made of. We are Texans and we will fight and die like proud Texans!

The boom from a distant cannon rolls across the landscape. The east wall buckles, killing several men.

It has begun.

Chapter 17: **It Begins and It Ends**

Travis immediately sends more men to the damaged east wall to fend off any Mexicans trying to enter through it.

The enemy continues to fire their cannons, punching holes in the rest of the walls and there is nothing we can do about it. Every time a cannonball fires, a wall starts crumbling.

Our men try shooting back but the enemy is just too far away.

I hear a voice yell, "Gunnar, get up here and show me what you can do that gun of yours!" I look to the top of the wall and see Davy Crockett waving me up. It's worth a try. I could probably kill more of from up there anyway. I climb and take my place with Davy Crocket. I aim my rifle and click off a shot. It hits one of the Mexicans dead center. I load up again and shoot again, killing another. But my efforts seem useless as cannonballs keep raining down over us. But I kept firing anyway and I kept killing more Mexicans.

There are just too many of them and not enough of us. Our men keep shouting for more water for our overheated rifles.

The Mexicans finally let up with their cannons.

We take the opportunity to load up our guns.

I hear a bugle and drum. They're signaling for the main attack.

"They're moving to the northwest corner!" someone shouts.

Their cannons begin firing at that wall, clearing the way for their soldiers to enter. Our men there didn't know what hit them.

I rush over to help.

I can see Bowie with his musket rifle, handgun and bowie knife by his side. He is ready to fight and die right where he stands.

The Mexican Army leans their ladders against a wall, but our men push it back down. Some of us are shot in the process. These are the same men I laughed and joked with and now I am seeing them die before my eyes. And I know this is just the beginning. Many more on both sides will die before this day is over.

The real fight has now begun as the Mexicans come over the wall. I fire my rifle and reload as quickly as I can but they just keep coming and coming. There are so many of them and we can't hold them off. Men are dying everywhere. But we keep reloading and keep shooting. I can't believe how brave these men are.

Three or four hours go by when suddenly, I hear a bugle playing and then that drum again. The Mexican Army is pulling back but our men keep shooting at them.

I think I'll go up the wall and kill some Mexicans as they retreat. My musket is loaded and ready to fire but then I stop because I see that they are helping their fallen soldiers back to safety.

I also see some women helping and a priest praying for those who have died. Part of me feels bad because I killed some of those men. But what else could I do? This is war and in war, men die. The motto is either you kill or get killed, and that's just the way it is.

Travis asks, "What are you waiting for?"

"I'm sure they would do the same for us."

I see a soldier carrying another. It would be an easy shot, too, but I help remove our wounded and dead from the wall instead.

Travis orders us to load all the muskets we have and to use all the Mexican rifles we can collect as well. "I'm sure they'll be back soon so we've got to be ready," he shouts.

"Gunnar, I'm starting to like you."

"Why?"

"When a man is down, you don't kick him. That's what separates us from the animals. I can see why Bowie likes you. You are a good fighter." He reaches into his pocket and pulls out a silver dollar. "You are worth your weight in gold out here and I want you to have this. This place and all these men have meant the world to me."

He goes to help with the wounded.

I load my guns and pick up rifles from some dead Mexicans.

As I walk down the line, I see some of my fellow Texans writing their last letters before they die here at the Alamo. Some are to their wives and others maybe to their girlfriends they left at home.

Looking over the wall, I can see that the Mexican Army is getting ready to attack us again.

Their cannons resume firing and cannonballs impact all around us. One hits close to me and knocks me down. The men nearby look at me with confusion as to why I didn't get hurt. They don't know I am protected by a force field.

I pick up my musket and get back into position, waiting for the cannonballs to stop coming down.

Their bugle sounds off again and their drum starts. The Mexican Army slowly marches side by side toward the Alamo. Many rows of determined Mexicans approach and it seems there's no stopping them. We all fire their muskets at them, but they just keep coming.

This is it. The final chapter and a fight to the end.

I'm down to old Sally. It's faster for me to use one gun anyway.

They're a lot closer to now. We continue to shoot them down but they're still firing back and we're losing a lot of men, too. Hundreds of bullets are being shot at the same time from both sides. And behind the front line, even more Mexicans fire and more Texans go down.

With ladders in hand, they prepare to mount the walls.

They keep coming and I keep putting more bullets into my musket but they're still pouring over the walls.

There's no stopping them now.

As I raise my head to shoot, I can feel many bullets ricocheting off of my face, thanks to my force field.

I see Travis up on the wall as a Mexican soldier is about to shoot him in the back. Bowie sees this and throws his knife at the Mexican and sticks him in the neck.

Travis looks over to Jim but before he could thank him, a Mexican shoots Jim Bowie dead. My heart stops for a moment, but there was just nothing I could do to save him. In that instant, I forgave him for whipping and killing his slave, Enu.

A Mexican soldier whips out his knife and runs it through William Travis. He looks to me as he falls from the wall.

Out of bullets, Davy Crockett fights the Mexicans with his empty gun, swinging it madly at the soldiers all around him. Finally, Davy is shot and falls dead.

I yell, "Viva, Davy Crockett!"

There was no greater man than he, and I'm sure he will always be remembered, even well beyond my time.

Standing on the plaza, I see Steve on the wall loading his musket. He takes aim at a barrel of gun power we use for the cannons. He fires at it and it explodes, killing a group of Mexicans.

As he loads his rifle again, a Mexican shoots him dead.

On the wall, Raquel's husband is shot twice in the chest but just manages to pull his knife and stab a Mexican before he falls. Lying on the ground he yells, "I love you, Raquel!" before he dies.

Watching all of this, I realize that I am now a part of its history.

But I think perhaps I need to leave now because a lot of bullets are hitting me in the front, side and back of my buckskin. The Mexicans want me dead but my force field won't let them get their way.

I think I am the last one alive.

Many Mexican soldiers are looking at me now and coming at me. I shout to them, "Now we're going play baseball without a ball. If you want a piece of me, come and get it! I'm standing right here and I'm not going anywhere. I'm a Texas bad-ass like you've never seen!"

They start shooting at me but I just pick up their bullets and throw them back, laughing. Charging at me, I swing old Sally hard at them, one after another, for what they did to my friends here.

But there are too many now to fight alone, so I push my ring and everybody stops. Before me, my time machine appears. I walk around the Mexican soldiers to see my dead friend, William Travis. I close his eyes and say, "I'm sorry for the way I spoke to you."

190

I then walk to my friend, Jim Bowie. I collect the knife he killed a soldier with and put it back into his holster.

And I go to my friend, Steve, and I close his eyes, too. I guess we will never go hunting after all.

I wish I could have told you all that I was a time traveler but you would not have believed me. I will die in time but I will not die today. It's now time to go back to my world. I walk to my time machine and the door opens for me. I go in and program the time for the future.

In a blink, the devastated environment around me transforms into an older-looking, but clean tourist attraction.

I get out and the entire city with all its people freezes. I go around and put my buckskin clothes in the trunk. I push my ring and my time machine disappears.

I go into a hotel. At the front desk is a pretty girl. She smells so good. It's been a long time since I've met someone that smelled good. At the Alamo, no one ever took a bath.

"I want a room for the night."

"Sign in, please."

I then realize that she is reacting to my own bad smell.

She gives me a key. A man comes up and she tells him, "Take Mr. Best to room 207."

We arrive and he asks, "Is there anything else, sir?"

"No thanks." I give him five dollars and he leaves.

I take a much needed shower and go to sleep for the night. I get up and feel much better. I go downstairs for some decent food.

While eating my eggs, I realize that I am surrounded by tourists. They must have gotten off a bus to come visit the Alamo. Everyone is talking about it. A fellow with two younger men seated with him says, "Ah, Bowie was a drunk and was cruel to his slaves and women."

I get up from my table, walk over and say, "Sir, you're talking bad about Jim Bowie and don't like it."

"You may not like it, but it's still true."

"I want you to say you're sorry and I don't ever want you to say anything like that again about him."

He replies, "I can see you know nothing about Jim Bowie or you would not say that to us. Besides, there are three of us and only one of you, so I suggest you leave before you get yourself hurt."

"I do not think so. I don't care how many of you there are. I can take one, two or three of you on any day of the week. I have a lot of respect for Jim. He died at the Alamo a national hero. He fought and gave his life for something he believed in and I respect any man who can do that for his country. So I will always honor his memory."

The men say nothing, but their faces show enough shame for me to know they're sorry, so I leave them.

I walk down the street. It's hard, but the Alamo was my home for a brief time and all my friends did die there. I stand before it now, building the courage to face what I will find inside.

I go in.

I think of my time here. Some days were bad but most were good. I see Jim Bowie's knife and Davie Crockett's musket. But most of all, I see all of my friends alive and dead all around in my mind's eye.

I can only stand it for a few minutes before I have to leave.

Outside, I find a bench and sit. I think about everything that has happened and get very depressed. So I lie down.

The next thing I know, it's dark. I must have fallen asleep.

I get up and walk back to my hotel.

I am approached by ten young men who block my path.

"What are you doing here in our side of town?" one of them asks.

"Your side of town?"

"This is going to cost you."

"No way. You will never get my money and live to talk about it. If you want a fight me, I'm ready." They put their fists up. "Get ready for a lot of pain coming your way."

One guy pulls a knife. I pull out mine. He says, "Hey, that's a big knife to be carrying around."

192

"I didn't know there were rules here. This knife's a good one, too. I call her old Sally and she really knows how to kill."

They start looking at each other funny.

"I killed lot of men out here. I fought alongside Davie Crockett, Jim Bowie and William Travis. A man you don't know named Steve was my best friend. He died here, too. I was the last man standing at the Alamo."

"Man, you're so full of shit, your eyes are brown!"

"It don't matter what you think of me. But I wanted you to know the truth. I was here in the year 1836. Now here I am again, about to fight all of you to the death. I fought four-thousand Mexican soldiers and they could not kill me but you want to try for my money. Well, good luck with that. One thing I can promise is that I won't be the one to die. All of you will die here instead and that's a promise. So who wants to die first?"

An ugly guy pulls a gun, points it at me and fires. When he sees the bullet do nothing to me, he runs away. I throw old Sally at him. She sticks him in the back and he goes down. I start hitting the other guys like I was at the Alamo fighting four thousand men. They have never seen a man fight like this before.

When I'm finished, some of them are dead and some are in a lot of pain. One of them pleads, "Help us. Please, sir."

"I'll help you. But next time, think before you start a fight with someone." I call 911 on their behalf.

I push my ring and there is my time machine. The door opens and as I look over to the young men who have stopped moving.

It's finally time to go back home to El Sobrante. Let's go, Nelly. I pull back on my steering wheel, set all the controls on my dashboard computer, and we're off.

Over the skies of California, I look down to my home far below as I slowly descend.

I get out of my time machine and the door closes. I walk into the house and there is my brother and Debbie in the kitchen.

"Hello, everybody. It sure is nice to be back."

"Welcome home," Debbie says.

"Brother," I tell James, "You are a great cook. I had to say that. I realized this back at the Alamo when trying to eat the food there."

He asks, "So how was it back at the Alamo in 1836?"

"It was hard to see people you know die before your eyes. But it was good to make friends with people that you only read about."

"But haven't you had enough of people trying to kill you all the time and seeing all your friends die?" Debbie asks.

I open my mouth to argue her point when it occurs to me that she is right. At the end of all my travels, it seems I always meet death.

"When I started all of this, life was a boring routine. After I got my time machine, life was an adventure. Maybe too much adventure. Now, it occurs to me that a boring life may be preferable."

James adds, "We're never happy with what we've got."

"I may change my mind, but I think my next adventure will be the next pretty girl I meet at the mall. Life is filled with enough problems and pleasures as it is. My time machine let me escape that. Maybe it's time I started really living life for a change."

www.ingramcontent.com/pod-product-compliance
Lightning Source LLC
Chambersburg PA
CBHW020606250626
47154CB00004B/1384